> Brooke,
> You're not on[ly a] reader, but a [model?]
> of kindness and caring for people.
> Although the former is awesome, it's
> the latter that makes me in awe of you.

DEMON EVOLUTION

Book Two of the

Evolution Trilogy

David Estes

Copyright © 2011 David Estes

All rights reserved.

ISBN-10: 1466422874
ISBN-13: 978-1466422872

Jacket concept by Adele Estes
Jacket art by Phatpuppy Art
Jacket design by Winkipop Design

This book is dedicated to my mother, Nancy,

for being my first-draft reader,

sounding board and supporter, and

for instilling in me the love for a good story.

PART I

"You say you gotta go and find yourself
You say that you're becoming someone else
Don't recognize the face in the mirror looking back at you
You say you're leaving as you look away
I know there's really nothing left to say
Just know I'm here whenever you need me, I will wait for you

So I'll let you go, I'll set you free
And when you've seen what you need to see
When you find you...come back to me"

David Cook- "Come Back to Me"
From the album *David Cook (2010)*

One

Being reunited with him was the sweetest feeling that Taylor had ever experienced, which she was loathe to admit. He had harmed her. Deeply, emotionally. But that didn't matter now. As Gabriel held her in his arms, the electricity of his embrace flowed through her like a fast-acting drug. By the time it reached her legs, she felt like she was floating. Maybe she was. Taylor looked down to see the ground moving away from her quickly, as Gabriel's snowy-white wings propelled them upwards.

"But where did you…how did you—?" Taylor started to ask.

Still gripping her firmly with one arm, Gabriel used the other arm to raise his index finger to her lips, to silence her. Removing his finger, he kissed her passionately on the lips, as they hovered thousands of feet from the distant earth below.

Momentarily drunk from the emotion of the kiss, Taylor struggled to remember where they were, how they got there—what question was she trying to ask him seconds earlier? The temporary intoxication waned and clarity returned to her mind. *Wait a minute*, she thought. *Something wasn't right.*

In a cliché act of truth-seeking, Taylor pinched herself hard on the arm. *Nothing.* She felt nothing. Not wanting it to end, she clung to Gabriel and hugged him fiercely. Despite her efforts, his perfect body began to fade—first his strong arms and legs, then his sculpted torso, until all that was left was his beautiful smiling face, framed by his wavy sandy-blond hair and strong chin. With nothing left to hold on to, Taylor dropped from the sky, plummeting towards the earth below. She was barely able to read his lips as she fell.

"I still love you," Gabriel's bodiless head mouthed.

Two

Grudgingly, Taylor awoke from the dream and sat up, slowly rubbing her eyes. "I still love you, too," she found herself whispering. "No I don't," she reminded herself. It wasn't that she wasn't a forgiving person. She was. But Gabriel had scarred her in more ways than one. His lies had been unforgivable, but she had forgiven him already. After all, he would be making the ultimate sacrifice for her: dying a traitor's death.

What she couldn't come to terms with was how he had changed her. By the end, she was no more than a trophy on his arm, a tool to be used mercilessly, a mere shadow of the independent girl her mother had taught her to be. The last time she was with him she almost died because of him.

Her mind wandered back to her dream from four months earlier, in which she had seen Gabriel for the first time. Gabriel's explanation tumbled through her head as vividly as if it were yesterday: "One of my abilities is to alter the dreams of any human I choose," he had said.

Taylor wondered if her own subconscious had created this dream—she hoped not—or if Gabriel was trying to communicate with her. She wondered where he was, what he was thinking. She hadn't seen him in nearly two weeks and, despite Christopher's reassurances, she feared he was dead. Angel prison was not a place you wanted to be, especially after being charged with treason, for which the penalty was death.

While her head warned her to steer clear of him, her heart hadn't given up the fight yet. *Hearts*, she thought, *what a nuisance*. No matter how hard she tried to listen to only her brain, her heart fought back like a cornered animal, yearning for Gabriel's touch. She knew she would give him a second chance—or maybe it was a third—if he didn't die first.

If Gabriel *had* forced himself into her dream, then it meant he was still alive, but for some reason Taylor was unable to draw any hope from the thought. The dream only made her miss him more. She needed to get back to the Lair, or she was going to go crazy. There was only one problem: her father.

"Taylor! C'mon down, I think you've slept in enough already, it's Christmas morning for goodness sake!" Her dad's voice carried up the stairs, down the hall, and straight through her bedroom door. She cringed.

"Okay, Eddie! I'll be right down!" she yelled back. How had she forgotten it was Christmas? Given everything that had happened to her in the last two weeks, she was entitled to be a bit less interested in the holidays than usual, but completely forgetting? That was unprecedented.

Nevertheless, she would be required to put on a happy face and participate in the festivities with her family, so as to not raise any unnecessary suspicion. She needed her dad in a good mood before she hit him with the question she had been procrastinating asking him.

Given his history of being extremely overprotective, Taylor doubted her father would easily agree to her plans to go on a beach vacation with her best friend and college roommate, Samantha. Of course, if he knew the real plan—to spend the school holidays in a dark cave network nicknamed "the Lair" with a bunch of demons, while trying to help her boyfriend, who happened to be an angel, escape from angel prison—there would be zero chance of gaining his approval.

Knowing her dad, she would need to concoct a reasonable and believable lie, and launch it at exactly the right time and in the right way. Easier said than done.

Before she could make a move to get out of bed, the cell phone sitting on her bedside table blared Pearl Jam's *Alive*, in response to an incoming call. She grabbed her phone and checked the caller—it was Samantha. Sam was the only other human who knew about her plight. In fact, given Sam's serious relationship with Christopher Lyon, a surprisingly well-mannered demon, she had become deeply involved in Taylor's situation.

Sam had been a rock throughout the ordeal, providing comfort, laughs, a shoulder to cry on, and anything else that Taylor needed. It was comforting for Taylor not to have to keep any secrets from her childhood friend.

"Hey, Sam," Taylor said.

"Merry Christmas!" Sam replied enthusiastically. "Why so glum, Tay? It's the happiest day of the year!" Taylor couldn't help but smile at her friend's energy. From the time they were kids, Sam had always believed in the magic of Christmas and seemed to truly believe that the holidays would somehow bring Taylor luck.

"Oh, I don't know, Sam. Maybe just the fact that my boyfriend has been kidnapped by some really nasty angels that want to cut him up into little pieces, which they will then burn just to be sure he doesn't put himself back together."

A few seconds of silence passed as it seemed Sam didn't know how to respond. "Look, Tay—" Sam began.

Taylor cut her off: "I'm sorry, I shouldn't have said that. I know you're just trying to make me feel better. It's just that I had a dream about him last night, and it's kind of put me in a rotten mood. It felt so real, like he had never left. I really miss that lying, flying jerk, Sam."

Sam laughed. "Funny how things change. It was always me that dated the jerks, but now I am with a gentleman."

"He's a demon, Sam."

"They're the good guys, remember?"

Admittedly, Taylor was still having trouble getting her head around the fact that the demons were trying to help save humankind, while the angels sought to destroy it. "I know," Taylor said.

Sam said, "But Gabriel showed he wants to be good, too. When he tried to save you. We *will* get Gabriel back. First, we need to get back to the Lair though. It just so happens I have some good news about that. My dad bought the story about Florida and he's letting me go as a reward for my grades this semester. He also said something like, 'Taylor is such a responsible girl.'"

Taylor laughed. "If only he knew the type of boys we've been hanging out with, he might change his tune," Taylor said.

"What did your dad say?"

"Umm…well, I haven't exactly told him yet."

"Tay! We are supposed to leave in three days, you need to tell him."

"I know, I know, I just haven't found the right time yet. I'll do it while we're opening Christmas presents this morning, so hopefully he'll be in a good mood. And you gave me a great idea: to use the good grades I got this semester as leverage."

An annoying voice came from the hallway. "Taylor, you seriously need to get off the phone and come downstairs; we've been waiting for you for hours."

James, Taylor's older brother, glared at her from the doorway. He had one foot in her room in an attempt to get under her skin. It worked.

"Get out of my room," Taylor demanded, standing up.

"Make me," James sneered.

"Sam, I gotta go, I have to call pest control."

"Okay, hun. Call me back as soon as you've talked to your dad."

"I will. Bye." She pressed the END button and returned her phone to her nightstand.

Turning her attention back to her infuriating brother, she considered giving him a real earful—telling him how full of himself he was and how his voice sounded like nails on a chalkboard. Instead, Taylor changed her mind, deciding that now was not the time to pick a fight with James. It would only put her father in a bad mood and lower her chances of getting his approval for her trip.

Laying on the sarcasm really thick, Taylor said, "Why thank you, James, for reminding me that I should be downstairs with my family on this beautiful Christmas morning."

James was unfazed by Taylor's attempt at civility. He suddenly darted into the room, tackling Taylor onto her bed. Before she could even curse at him, James had released her and was back out the door and running down the stairs laughing.

Taylor took two deep breaths and waited for her anger to subside. *I can get my revenge later*, she thought. Before making her way downstairs, she looked in the mirror. Ugh. Her brown hair was tangled and full of static. Her face was tired, with slightly sunken eyes and an unsettling weariness in her skin. She made eye contact with herself, her mild brown eyes probing into her consciousness through the looking glass, searching for something. Turning her shoulder, she was able to make out a portion of the dark tattoo that slithered across the upper left quadrant of her back. The red-eyed serpent had been etched in her skin when she was sixteen, as a symbol of conquered childhood fear. Once upon a time, as a little girl, she had been scared of closing her eyes. Plagued with a recurring nightmare about a deadly black snake that sought to end her existence, Taylor eventually—only after he mother died—cast aside her fear. The nightmares didn't stop, but she didn't fear them anymore.

Then Gabriel came along and slew the beast. Literally. He entered her nightmare and thrust a sword through her childhood monster's heart. She hadn't had a nightmare about the snake since. So she got another tattoo, on her ankle. Much smaller, the second bit of skin-art again featured the inky snake, but this time the serpent was strung up on a steel blade, limp and lifeless. Defeated and dead.

Shaking off the memory, Taylor focused on brushing the knots out of her messy hair. Then she went to her dresser and slipped on each of the nine rings that she wore on a daily basis. When she had met Gabriel, she wore only eight. Three days earlier, she had added the ninth, featuring a pair of angel wings. At the jewelry store, she had hesitated before buying the silver ring; she was worried that it was a sign of weakness, of dependency on Gabriel. But then she bought it anyway. To her it was more of a reminder to trust her instincts, what her mom used to refer to as her "good gut".

Not bothering to change out of her pajamas, Taylor made her way downstairs and into the kitchen. Entering the cooking area, she took a moment to breathe in the mouth-watering aroma of sausage, eggs and bacon. Despite all of her complaints about Eddie, she had to give him credit: he was an amazing cook.

"Wow, Dad, something smells delicious!" she exclaimed enthusiastically.

"Good morning, princess," he replied, kissing her on the forehead, "and Merry Christmas."

"Merry Christmas, Dad," she said, her voice catching in her throat. The hint of emotion that she felt took her by surprise.

With his usual dad-radar, Ed noticed the change in her voice and gave his only daughter a big hug. "I know. I miss her too, Taylor."

Taylor hugged him back tightly and tried not to tear up. Although her mother had died more than five years earlier, the pain still lingered, especially around the holidays.

She had died in a car accident, when a drunk driver ran a red light and collided with her front driver's side door. The medical examiner said that she had likely died instantly.

Nancy Kingston died while coming home from one of her business trips. Her flight had been delayed almost two hours and didn't land until ten o'clock at night. She was flying first-class and was probably one of the first people off of the airplane. Having only carry-on luggage, she would have made her way directly to her car and would have been on the highway by ten-twenty.

She had called home on the road to let her family know that there was construction on the I-5, and she was going to use her GPS to reroute through Dixon County, an area she was not particularly familiar with. Having successfully navigated through Dixon, her mother was only two miles from home when she crossed the normally busy intersection of Commander Street and Apache Avenue. At the late hour, the area was deserted and the traffic light showed a steady green in her favor.

Not giving it a second thought, Nancy would have cruised through the intersection, her mind carrying thoughts of seeing her family, having a hot shower and getting to bed. Evidently, she didn't notice the black truck, its headlights extinguished, bearing down on her left side—until it was too late.

A witness on a bike confirmed that the accident was the fault of the driver of the black truck and, given his blood-alcohol level was well over the legal limit, he was sentenced to manslaughter, which carried a prison term of five to seven years. But none of that made up for the unnecessary loss of life that had occurred.

Taylor's mother had been a highly respected expert on public speaking and had traveled around the country giving *Speak Out* seminars to help people overcome their fear of public speaking, as well as to help seasoned public speakers hone and perfect their skills. She had worked with many politicians and CEOs, and her funeral was attended by the who's who of the nation's government and business leadership.

Taylor often thought about how, if one small detail of her mother's day had changed, she wouldn't have arrived at that exact intersection, at that exact time. What if the plane wasn't delayed? Or delayed less? Or delayed more? What if she was stuck in the back of the plane and it took her a few minutes longer to escape into the terminal? What if there was no construction on the highway or she had just decided to suffer through it? At first, Taylor made herself crazy thinking about the what-ifs, but over time she thought about them less and less and tried to move on with her life, as her mom would want her to do.

Taylor's mom has been her hero, her confidante, and most importantly, her friend. Good memories of her mom swirled through her mind, but she quickly blocked them out as she knew it would only lead to tears.

Releasing her dad from the embrace, she said, "Let's eat."

Her father smiled and prepared three lots of food. James appeared just as his plate touched the table, like a bloodhound that had tracked a pungent scent. He smirked at his sister, but Taylor managed to ignore him as she took her first bite of food.

"Mmmm, this is great, Dad. If it were up to me, we would just skip the presents and eat all morning." While it felt like a lame attempt to butter him up before dropping the question, Taylor actually meant what she said. Presents were not really her thing. *Food was.*

James took the opportunity to take another shot at her: "We can tell, Taylor. It seems the dining hall buffets are catching up with you already. You do realize that you have a full year to gain the Freshman Fifteen, you didn't have to do it all in one semester!"

Taylor was on a mission and couldn't be side-tracked by James's antics. Impressing herself and her dad with her self-control, she ignored him and said to Eddie, "The sausages are especially good, did you do something different with them?"

Following her lead and ignoring James, Ed replied, "Thanks, Taylor, I'm glad you like it. I created a mixed spice and used it to season the sausage before frying it up."

"Well, whatever you did, it worked." Taylor grinned. In a spur of the moment decision, she blurted out, "Hey, Dad, I've been meaning to ask you. Me and Sam want to take advantage of the holidays and go on vacation with a couple of friends from school. Are you okay with me going?"

Seemingly surprised by the question, Ed paused before answering. Taylor added, "Sam's dad already said she could go as a reward for her good grades, perhaps you could think of it as sort of the same thing for me."

Taylor watched closely, as her father raised his arms and put them behind his head, and then tilted his head back to look at the ceiling. *Oh crap*, she thought, *this is not good*. Rare was the occasion when Eddie acted in this manner and then approved a request from one of his offspring. Usually it meant that he thought the idea was completely out of the question and he just needed a few minutes to think of the many reasons why he would reject it.

James's face broke into that annoying smirk that made Taylor want to slap him, as he waited for his dad to reject his sister's idea.

Shocking both of them, Ed's face suddenly broke into a smile and he said, "Merry Christmas, Taylor, you have my permission to go."

James's jaw dropped open and he protested, "Dad, you can't be serious, she's only eighteen and not that smart—"

Taylor was too happy to contradict her brother's insult. She got up and put her arms around Eddie's neck, the way she used to when she was a kid. "Thank you, Dad. This is the best Christmas gift ever." Not wanting to look a gift-horse in the mouth, but curious as to how she was able to gain his approval, she asked, "Is this a reward for something?"

"Sort of. Sam's father and I have been talking about giving you and Sam something to congratulate you guys on your first semester at college, especially given how good your grades were. He called me this morning and told me what Sam had asked him for, and he convinced me to trust you and your judgment, and let you go on this trip. There are, of course, a couple of requirements."

"Of course, anything you want, Dad."

"One: no boys are permitted. Two: you will call me every day without fail. And three: have fun and don't do anything stupid."

"I think I can handle those, I won't let you down."

"Good, now let's go open some presents."

Not wanting to interrupt the positive energy, Taylor sent a quick text to Sam to tell her the good news, and promised to call her later. The rest of the morning was spent giving and receiving gifts. Taylor had bought her dad a new watch that he had been talking about for weeks. For James, she presented a pair of weightlifting gloves, as he had been complaining that the heavier dumbbells "tore up his hands pretty good."

His response to the gift was to be expected, "Thanks, Sis, maybe you're not such a dork after all."

"I'll take that as a compliment," she replied. They both laughed, a rare moment of brother-sister bonding that was sure to be short-lived.

Besides permission to go on her trip, Eddie gave Taylor three gift cards—one to each of her favorite stores—an iPad, and a handful of CDs and DVDs that she had told him she wanted. James gave her a padlock for her bedroom door as a gag-gift and a newly released book by her favorite author. Happy with the successful morning, Taylor headed back upstairs to call Sam.

Three

Christopher put his cell phone down and smiled. Sam had just called to tell him the good news—she and Taylor were coming back to the Lair.

Originally, he had thought that some time away from Samantha would give them both a chance to do some things on their own. They had been spending so much time with each other, maybe some space would help their relationship strengthen further. Instead, every hour that passed without her was filled with emptiness and longing. Chris physically hurt inside when he was separated from her. Trying to fill his days with activities to take his mind off of Sam, Chris spent twelve hours a day coordinating the two top priorities as mandated by the demon Elders.

First, was the protection of Taylor, Sam, and their families. Around-the-clock security details maintained a close watch on them, but so far there had been no attempts by the angels to retrieve Taylor. Perhaps the Archangel Council realized that they had acted too hastily before, and now they were trying to be more patient in their plans. *There was no doubt that they would come for her again.* The only question was when.

The second priority was helping Gabriel escape from angel prison. It had taken Chris a significant amount of effort to convince the demon Elders that Gabriel was worthy of their help. Why should they help the angel that had provided the angel army with the most powerful weapon the world had ever seen? But Chris's eye-witness account of Gabriel's failed attempt to rescue Taylor, and his subsequent battle with Dionysus, the Head of the Archangel Council, was highly convincing proof that Gabriel could become an important ally in the War. It didn't hurt that Gabriel had been accused of treason against the angel cause. "Any enemy of the angels is a friend to the demons," Clifford, the head of the demon Elders, liked to say.

The end result was that Chris had been provided with what appeared to be endless resources to accomplish the demons' goals. He was also allowed access to top-secret information that would give him a chance to accomplish the seemingly impossible task of infiltrating the angels' underground prison.

It had come as quite a shock to Chris that there were actually angels acting as spies on behalf of the demons. In hindsight, it should have been expected. All throughout history, there are examples of people betraying their own kind for various reasons. Love, money, fame, to do the right thing: these were all possible reasons for disloyalty.

Regardless of their motives, these angel spies had become invaluable due to their ability to provide inside information to Chris, and to pass instructions to Gabriel. He hoped that all of the hard work was about to pay off. Picking up his cell phone and flipping it open, he pressed speed dial 9. When a voice answered, "Yessir," Chris barked, "Operation Traitor is a go." He snapped the phone shut and strode off towards an open transporter—it was waiting for him, ready to carry him to where the Elders were meeting.

Four

The last week had been a rush for Gabriel. Well, as much of a rush as life in imprisonment could be. Despite his lowly conditions—being stuck in a cold, gloomy, 12-foot by 12-foot stone box—he had felt a thrill each time he saw a folded scrap of paper flutter through the air hole in his cell door. After hearing nothing for almost a week, the communications were coming in on a daily basis now, evidence that plans were being ramped up and finalized. Based on the note he had received the previous day, it seemed that his rescue could come any day. The note, printed in the usual block letters, had read:

BE READY TO MOVE
THIS IS THE LAST COMM.
GOOD LUCK

Upon reading the most recent note, Gabriel had waited in anticipation, fighting off sleep until late into the night. Eventually he had succumbed to his body's need for rest and fell asleep for nearly ten hours, using his soft wings as a bed. He was awake again now, feeling full of energy and hoping desperately that today was the day.

Gabriel assumed that the attempt would be made at night and, given that he had received his meager dinner ration more than three hours earlier, he waited on his feet for any sign that help was coming.

An hour later, he was still waiting and beginning to consider sitting down again to rest his stiff legs, when a noise caught his attention. Typically, this late at night the prison was devoid of sound, as the handful of inmates slept in silence. There were no snorers in this bunch.

The sound was so soft that at first Gabriel thought he might have imagined it. But then he heard it again. A soft patter of a footstep, a scuff of a shoe on the rocky floor: someone was tiptoeing down the corridor, trying to muffle their presence.

Gabriel watched the door intently, ready to spring into action if needed. For all he knew it could be his executioner, and if so, he would fight like hell to protect himself. But some instinct told him that it was a friend, rather than a foe, and thus, he prepared himself to run and follow any instructions that were given.

The tread of footsteps ended abruptly and silence resumed. Gabriel strained to discern whether the visitor had stopped outside his cell. The clink of metal on metal: a key was inserted into a keyhole; *it was very close, it had to be his door*. Ever so slowly, without so much as a creak, his door opened. *Good old fashioned angel engineering,* Gabriel thought.

When the door was halfway open, a familiar face crowned by a fully white shock of hair popped through the opening and hissed, "Hey, cowboy, it's time to get the hell outta here!"

Gabriel stared at his friend in surprise. "Sampson? I never would have…I thought you were true blue angel all the way."

"If you want to stand here and discuss the pros and cons of treason, I'd be happy to, but then we'll have to share a cell when we get busted, and I really don't see us as being very good cellmates."

"Right, sorry, let's go!" Gabriel raced through the door and into the corridor.

Sampson noiselessly closed the door and whispered instructions to Gabriel as they snuck towards the exit. "The only guards on duty right now are *ours*. They'll ignore us like we don't even exist. Follow me at all times; there is only one way this is going to work."

"Won't those guards get charged with treason when the Council finds out I have escaped?" Gabriel asked.

"Maybe. That's a risk they've agreed to take, but it's likely that there won't be sufficient proof to charge them with anything."

They reached the prison gates and, without hesitation, Sampson unlocked and pushed them open. They turned to the right, down a passageway.

"Wait, Sampson! Where are we going? The way out is the other direction!"

"Didn't I just tell you to follow me? Trust me, there is a much better route, unless you want to pass through the highest-traffic areas just to make this a challenge?" Sampson joked.

"Maybe next time. I'll just follow you if that's alright?"

Sampson picked up the pace and they quickly reached full angel running speed, blazing down the tunnel much faster than a pair of humans could. Gabriel was hot on his heels as they followed the path deep into the mountain. He could easily follow his friend, who was built like a tank—shorter than him, but far denser. Along the way, they encountered several angel guards, each of whom pretended that they didn't see the pair of streaking angels fleeing down the tunnel. They passed many sealed doors that contained warnings of "Authorized personnel only," or "Restricted access," until the path finally reached a dead end—a rock wall blocked their progress.

"I told you, Sampson, there is no way out down here!" Gabriel snapped.

"Watch and learn, my friend," Sampson replied calmly.

Sampson took a few large steps back, and then charged directly towards the solid rock wall. Gabriel thought his friend had gone mad, but then, when his shoulder drilled into the rock, Sampson crashed straight through it, rather than getting thrown back like Gabriel had expected. The mountain shuddered from the impact and the surrounding attack sensors were tripped, causing loud alarm sirens to blare throughout the underground complex. *Their escape was no longer a secret.*

Gabriel followed his friend through the rock, where a hidden passageway had been revealed. Sampson said, "We dug it just for you, buddy, now let's not waste it by getting caught!"

The pair flew down the tunnel, their feet barely touching the ground.

Five

Taylor heard her father answer the door. She was in her room packing, but his booming voice easily carried up the staircase.

"Hi, Sam," he said.

"Hey, Mr. Kingston," Sam replied. "How was your Christmas?"

"It was great, Sam, although I think I've spent about 10 hours over the last two days trying to set up the new surround-sound system that James bought me."

Sam laughed. "Electronics never were your strong suit," she said.

"No, I suppose not," he replied. "Taylor's in her room finishing packing. You can leave your suitcase here until she's finished."

"Thanks, Mr. K," Sam said. Taylor heard her friend's footsteps marching up the stairs.

Sam entered her room and flashed a model-perfect smile in a flurry of shimmering blond hair and lots of legs, highlighted by what Taylor would consider an overly short skirt. Taylor said loudly, "I am nearly done packing, but first I need your advice on which bikini to take."

"Taylor, we're not really going to need—" Sam started to respond.

Taylor gave her friend an icy look and asked loudly, "This one or this one?" She held up one black swimsuit and one red.

Catching on, Samantha raised her voice and responded, "Why not take them both, Tay?"

"Great idea," Taylor said, throwing them both in her suitcase. She zipped it shut and said, "That's it, let's go."

Taylor hauled her suitcase down the stairs to the door, where Eddie was waiting for them. Before he could open his mouth, Taylor said, "Don't worry, Dad. We'll both be very careful and I will call you every day as I promised I would."

Taylor's dad gave a wry smile and said, "And no boys, right?"

"Of course, Dad, see you in a couple of weeks." Feeling somewhat bad about having to lie, she gave him a quick kiss on the cheek.

Following the girls outside, Mr. Kingston said, "Drive safe, Sam."

"I will. Bye, Mr. Kingston."

"Bye, girls."

Once they were on the road and heading for the airport, Taylor felt it was finally safe to speak openly. "Any news from Chris on the mission?" she asked.

"Why don't you ask him yourself?" Sam replied.

"What?" Taylor asked, puzzled. Then she screamed, as a pair of hands covered her eyes from behind, temporarily obscuring her vision.

"Guess who?" a deep voice asked from the back seat.

Pulling his hands from her face, Taylor whipped her head around. A black-haired stud with two days-worth of rugged stubble was looking at her. "Geez, Chris, you practically gave me a heart attack."

"Sorry about that. I just thought I should come along to personally transport you back to the Lair."

"Thanks, but that was really unnecessary. Any of the other demons could have done it. You should really be helping with the *other* mission. You know, the important one?"

"We should tell her, Chris," Sam interjected.

"Tell me what?" Taylor asked slowly.

"Well, it's nothing really. Your safety has just become a bigger risk, so I wanted to see to it that you made it back without any problems," Chris said cryptically.

"We haven't seen a single evil angel since we've arrived home, why would we be in danger?"

"I received a report from one of Sam's security guards ten minutes ago. It seems that an angel scout followed Sam over to your house. As soon as I received the report, I teleported into her car."

Sam said, "Yeah, you think you were scared when he put his hands over your eyes, Tay? Imagine driving along, when a dark form suddenly appears next to you. I practically swerved off the road into a tree."

"What are we going to do about the damn angel scout?" Taylor said.

"Nothing yet. As long as he keeps his distance, we will just stick with the original plan: Park Sam's car at the airport and then teleport from there."

A scratchy voice suddenly spoke from the backseat. It came from Chris's radio. "Chris, we have a situation here. Two other angels have joined the scout and they are flying above you, following your car. How should we handle it?"

Chris said firmly, "Take them down."

"Consider it done," the voice confirmed.

"Shoot," Chris said. "That was our rear guard. They are following behind us in a car, but will have to stop to get rid of those angels. The car in front of us is also full of demon guards though, so we should still be protected."

Six

Gabriel and Sampson burst through the end of the tunnel together, their shoulders lowered to absorb the impact of the thin rock wall that had been enacted to disguise the entrance.

Once outside, Gabriel paused to gulp down deep breaths of fresh air. "Ahhh," he sighed.

"This is no time to stop and smell the roses," Sampson said. "We gotta get outta here now!" In near-perfect synchronization, the two angels' wings burst from the base of their necks and majestically spread into a V. They leapt high into the air and powered away from the earth in a burst of light, harnessing the energy of the full moon.

But they were too late.

The attack came from above and the impact was mind-numbing, like a sledge hammer to the head. One angel collided with Gabriel and another slammed into Sampson. Three or four more angel attackers piled onto each of them, swiftly tying their wings together with glowing ropes, rendering them useless. Their arms were also bound behind their backs before the squad of angels carried them back to the earth.

Knowing they would both be put to death, Gabriel and Sampson fought like cornered animals, but with only the use of their legs, they were no match for the strong angels, and were quickly wrestled to the ground and subdued.

"You're gonna pay for this one," the leader of the group sneered. He was young, probably no older than Gabriel, and athletic-looking—Gabriel could see his lean, sinewy muscles straining through his shirt. His mouth formed a snarl.

Sampson gritted his teeth and said, "You'll get what's coming to you, Lucas."

Somehow Lucas's mouth widened into a smile while maintaining the snarl. He laughed, deep and throaty. "Now that's the funniest thing I've heard in my entire life. I am going to build my career off of the back of your mistakes, Sampson, and the mistakes of Gabby here." He turned to Gabriel. "You would've been a star, but instead you're a dead man, and I'm the rising star."

Gabriel stared at him, unspeaking.

Lucas was about to unload another threat when Gabriel saw a flash of fire come from the side, barely within the spectrum of his peripheral vision. Lucas's reflexes were up to the challenge; in less than a second, he was wielding a dazzlingly bright sword, raising it swiftly to thwart off the incoming attack. Despite the speed of his defense, Lucas was thrown back by the deafening metal-on-metal impact of the fiery sword against his own.

Moments later, there were a dozen bursts of fire around the group, as the demon special-attack force surrounded them, brandishing flaming swords and shields. The angels moved into formation to prevent their captives from being rescued—their brilliant swords lit up in response to the attack. With a yell of "Attack!" from one of the demons, probably the mission leader, the battle began. The clash of swords sounded like thunder in the night and, for someone watching from the distance, it would have looked like a small fireworks display.

The angels were mercilessly outnumbered and during the hand-to-hand combat one of the demons was able to slip through their defenses and slash the ropes away from Gabriel and Sampson. They were free, again.

Sampson immediately drew his sword, but the demon that had freed them said, "This is not your fight, I will get you out of here."

Seeing the wisdom in this, Sampson replied, "Okay. Gabriel, get over here."

Gabriel was gazing at the battle, debating whether to jump into the fray, despite not having a weapon other than his bare hands. "Give me your sword, Sampson," he commanded.

"Gabriel, there will be a time and a place to get your revenge. But now we must escape."

Gabriel watched as Lucas struck down the demon he was fighting. He thrust his sword directly into the heart of his struggling victim. With a look of pure hatred, he stared at Gabriel and pointed his sword at him. For Gabriel, retreating from a fight with Lucas was the hardest thing he had ever had to do in his life. Every instinct was telling him to destroy the rival angel, but instead he listened to his friend, who had risked his life to help him escape.

Just before Gabriel was teleported from the battle, he saw Lucas raise his arm and slash his thumb across his neck. Gabriel understood the message: "I'm going to kill you." It didn't bother him though, because he was thinking the same thing.

Seven

Taylor watched as Sam gripped the wheel harder, her knuckles turning white from the pressure. By applying more force to the accelerator, she had managed to stay close to the lead car when it sped up in response to the reports about the angel pursuers. Taylor had never seen her friend this nervous—typically she was highly confident, bordering on cockiness at times.

The road they were on was quiet—no one was outside and they were the only cars on the road. That's when they lost their last line of defense.

One moment the lead car was zooming along, about three car-lengths in front of them, and the next moment it erupted in a ball of fire when a basketball-sized pulse of light struck it, like a heat-seeking missile finding its target. The car flew thirty feet in the air before landing in a heap on one of the well-manicured front lawns they were passing.

Samantha screamed and tried to swerve, but she couldn't avoid driving directly through the wall of fire that rose from the road. Luckily, the car was moving fast enough to slice through the flames and emerge on the other side unscathed, but due to the lack of visibility and Sam's sudden turn of the wheel, the car jumped the curb and clipped a fire hydrant. They came to rest on the sidewalk and, amidst a shower from the burst hydrant, Chris jumped out and pulled a stunned Samantha from the car. He re-belted her into the backseat and took over as driver.

Chris gunned the engine, reversed, and then accelerated quickly, spraying rubber on the curb, as he tore back onto the road. "Are they dead?" Taylor asked, referring to the demons in the lead car.

"No, they should be fine," Chris replied. "A little banged up maybe, but a little fire doesn't hurt our kind."

"What the hell was that?" Taylor said.

Chris answered in one word: "Angels."

"I know that, but does it mean they defeated the demon guard?"

"I don't know. Let's find out," Chris replied.

Pumping the radio to his mouth, he barked, "Rear guard, what is your status?"

The radio crackled and they heard, "Mission complete. We teleported onto the angels' backs and were able to force them to land. But then one of our men grabbed them and teleported them to who knows where. Adrian is a traitor, sir."

"Okay, there's nothing we can do about that now. We've been attacked by a second group of angels. Can you and one of your squad members teleport to our vehicle? We are about two blocks down Crown Street."

Seconds later, they heard a thud on the roof of their car. "Sam, move to the middle seat," Chris ordered. Obediently, his girlfriend undid her belt and slid over. After rolling down his window, Chris shouted, "C'mon in!"

Even though she would have been expecting it, Sam visibly twitched when the demons suddenly appeared on each side of her. "Hiya, Sam," one of them said.

"Hey, Chuck," she replied. Charles Booth was a close friend of Chris's, and both Samantha and Taylor had talked to him a few times before. Charles, or Chuck as most of the demons called him, was an intelligent, but fit-looking demon, with dark black eyes and sharp eyebrows that made him appear to be intensely concentrating. He was also highly handsome—he kind of reminded Taylor of the smart but sexy Dr. Karev from *Grey's Anatomy*.

Taylor didn't know the other demon who had appeared, but she looked strangely familiar. Her hair was a bright shade of green, which contrasted sharply to her shadowy aura. "Hi, I'm Kiren. I don't think we've been formally introduced," she said, extending her hand.

Taylor shook her hand while looking at her curiously. "Taylor. Do I know you from somewhere?"

Kiren laughed. "Sort of. I go to the University of Trinton with you guys, too. I actually live on the same floor as you in Shyloh Hall. My roommate is your friend—Marla."

"Seriously? Sorry, I should have known," Taylor said.

"No, no, don't worry. I came to UT just to keep an eye on you and Chris, and I was instructed to lay low. I hope I didn't freak Marla out too much, she seems like a sweet girl."

It was Sam's turn to laugh. "Well, I think she would like a roommate that actually talks to her and doesn't come out only at night, but other than that I think she loves you as her roommate."

Kiren's eyebrows wrinkled into a frown. "I guess I might have overplayed the strange and mysterious vibe a little bit. I'll try to be more social next semester, especially now that my cover is blown anyway."

Taylor was happy for some light conversation to take her mind off of the near-death experience they had just had. Her distraction was short lived, however, as she was jolted back to reality when Chris cried out, "We've got company, hang on!" Yanking the wheel hard to the left, he fish-tailed the car onto a side street, just as a ball of light struck the road in front of them.

The passengers turned around to gawk out the back window. Three white cars made the same turn behind them, in hot pursuit. "Uh, Chris," Chuck said, "they've got better wheels than us."

"Yeah, thanks for pointing that out," Chris retorted. He was driving Sam's red 2009 Honda Civic Hybrid. Not a bad little car, and great for the gas mileage, but it was no match for the souped up vehicles that were chasing them. In fact, Taylor wasn't sure that a jet would be any match for the angels' rides: A Porsche, Ferrari, and Lamborghini cruised down the road behind them in a rare display of beauty and power that would surely draw the gaze of anyone within sight. They needed to get to the highway.

Kiren opened her window and pulled her narrow body through it. She looked back at their pursuers. "Incoming!" she yelled. Taylor watched as another orb of light pulse from the white Porsche. The top was down, making it easier for the angels to fire off light attacks.

Chris slammed his foot down hard on the accelerator, trying to outrun the ball of light. Thrusting her hand out, Kiren was barely able to maintain her balance by clutching the side of the car, while precariously dangling from the window. At the same time, she fired her own weapon: three boulder-like balls of fire bounced down the road. The first collided with the orb, in an explosion of fire and light. The smoke and fire from the blast temporarily blocked their rear vision, but it also allowed the remaining two boulders of fire to charge towards their pursuers unseen.

At the exact moment when the white Porsche cut through the smokescreen, the fiery cannonball struck its front bumper. Like a lever, the car was flipped high into the air and then, reaching its peak, arced downwards, landing on top of the next car in the line—the Ferrari—stopping it dead in its tracks. The final pursuer deftly maneuvered around the mangled white metal of its two predecessors, but met a similar fate when the third and final fire boulder hurtled into its side, leaving the Lamborghini incapacitated.

"Three for three—not bad," Kiren said, as she pulled herself back through the window.

"That was amazing," Sam said, clearly in awe.

Kiren grinned from ear to ear. "Nice work, Kiren," Chris said.

"No problem," she replied.

Taylor looked in the rear-view mirror at the female demon sitting beside Sam. She hadn't really paid much attention to her appearance when they first met, but now, after seeing what she was able to do, Taylor couldn't help but stare. She was of average height, her muscles toned, but not too bulky. While her green hair was cut short, like a boy, it was styled—spiky in all directions—giving her a kind of punk rock star look. Her smile was cute, infectious even. Taylor turned her attention back to the road, thankful that for the moment they weren't being pursued.

Two streets later, they were on the highway and headed for the airport. While it would be easier to simply teleport from where they were, they needed to maintain the charade that they were taking a trip to Florida, just in case. Ten minutes later, they pulled into the airport parking lot and quickly found a spot as far away from any other cars as possible.

"Okay. Chuck, you teleport Sam and I'll teleport Taylor. Kiren, you're on your own." Chris gave orders like they were in the military—he was still in mission mode.

They held hands with their teleport buddies and, after a few seconds of the tell-tale swirling-twisting-flipping feeling, they appeared in a dark room with many rising seats in a U-shape on three sides of them. Dark men and women stopped in mid-conversation to inspect the new arrivals. Taylor had never been to the place before, but the rest of them had.

"Hi, Cliff," Sam said energetically.

Her remark was directed at a particularly old demon, who was standing at a raised podium, set off from the other seats. While he showed clear signs of aging, he was still a very handsome man, like Sean Connery, or Bob Barker, with a full head of dark hair and a well-kept beard. He smiled at Samantha. "Ahh, my dear, how nice of you to return to us. And you've brought your friend, I see."

"This is Taylor," she said, with a wave of her hand.

Taylor waved casually.

"Welcome to the Eldership of the demons," Clifford said grandly.

"Thank you," Taylor said. She had been in a similar situation before, but in a room full of *angel* leaders. That hadn't turned out too well, so she was wary of her current situation.

"Now...," Clifford started to say.

Taylor cut him off: "Have you rescued Gabriel yet?"

Clifford looked at Taylor with pain in his eyes. "The mission was going according to plan, but then we received reports that, while they were making their escape, Gabriel and his escort were recaptured by a contingent of particularly nasty angels. A few minutes before you arrived, we sent our special-attack squad to try to save them, but we haven't heard back from them yet. We are beginning to fear the worst."

"No!" Taylor yelled. "Send another squad; you can't let them take him. They're going to kill him." She felt her muscles tense under her clothing. Sweat beaded on her forehead, although she wasn't warm. Images of Gabriel whipped through her mind like a whirlwind: Gabriel sitting in a dark cell; Gabriel being taunted by the angel guards; and finally, Gabriel being murdered, his body burned to prevent him from pulling himself back together.

Eight

Bodies crashed into bodies, like a game of Twister gone horribly wrong. Someone screamed. Then, like a row of dominos, they collapsed in a heap of flesh.

Taylor had the wind knocked out of her when a large body landed on her. Gasping for breath, she croaked, "Get the hell off of me." That's when she saw the blood, black and pooling—demon blood. "Help!" she yelled as loudly as she could.

In response to her plea, the lifeless body was lifted from her small frame by two hands. The hands were strong. And familiar, somehow. The hands said, "Take him." *That voice*, she thought.

The body was passed to a second pair of hands and a face came into view. "Taylor," the face said.

Just another dream. Gabriel's beautiful face peered down at her and he reached for her hand. "You can't keep doing this to me," Taylor said. "I have to learn to let you go."

Gabriel looked puzzled. "What do you mean?" he asked. He grabbed her hand, pulling her up.

His touch felt so good, so real. Taylor looked around her. She was still in the room with the rising chairs. She saw Chris helping Sam to her feet, and a dozen other demons were in the room now. Something was different about this dream. Taylor was afraid to hope, but still….She pinched herself hard on the arm. "Oww!" she exclaimed.

Gabriel looked amused. Taylor reached out and pinched him equally hard. "Ouch!" he yelped. "What did you do that for?"

Taylor's muscles tensed again, but not in anger or frustration…in anticipation. Wrapping her arms around him, she hugged Gabriel tightly, as if anything less would allow him to disappear. "I thought I'd lost you," she whispered.

Gabriel tilted her head back to look into her eyes. He said, "I thought I'd lost your love."

"You should have," she said, an edge creeping into her voice.

"Why didn't I?" Gabriel asked.

"I don't know," Taylor said honestly. A sudden rage surged through her. She had the desire to punch him, to kick him, to swear at him. He had hurt her so badly, he deserved to be hurt too. He *had* been hurt, she reminded herself. His punishment had been sufficient.

Abruptly, Taylor noticed that everyone in the room was watching them now, but she continued to hold Gabriel fiercely, afraid to let go. She spotted Sampson, and her eyes widened. "But what—? What are you doing here?"

His face bursting into a massive smile, Sampson said, "Oh, come on now. You didn't think I would leave Gabriel all by himself, did you?"

Taylor smiled back. "No, I guess not," she said.

Clifford approached them and said to Gabriel, "We have much to discuss, young angel, but first you should eat…and rest."

"Thank you," Gabriel said. "Thank you for everything."

Nine

"Whose body was that?" Taylor asked. Taylor, Gabriel, Sam, Chris, and Sampson were in the demon café watching Gabriel inhale a massive plate of food. They had already eaten. Gabriel was working on his third plate.

Gabriel looked up from his feeding, like a pig above its slop bucket. "I dunno. Chris?"

Keeping his voice even, Chris said, "It was Dom. He was dead before they even got him to the medical center. He was a friend of mine." Samantha put her arm around her boyfriend's back and pulled him towards her.

"Oh, Chris, I'm so sorry," she said.

"Who killed him?" Chris asked.

Gabriel finished chewing the mouthful he was working on and replied, "A filthy angel named Lucas. He is the Archangel Council's new toy. They will try to use him to kill me and abduct Taylor. But I'm going to kill him first."

Taylor frowned. "That would be stupid, considering you've just been rescued."

Chris interjected, "Don't worry, we won't be doing anything right away. The Elders will need to discuss the situation and decide what to do next. For now, no one is going anywhere."

The scowl that had formed on Gabriel's face when he was talking about Lucas lingered for a moment, and then dissipated, as he resigned himself to the fact that he needed to involve the demons in any plans going forward. "Fair enough," he said. "Besides, I have everything I need right here." He smiled at Taylor, although she continued to frown at him.

Samantha asked, "What happened in the Elder's room, anyway?"

Chris laughed. "Remember when I told you that all teleporting in and out of the Lair is carefully controlled?" She nodded. "Well, that is why we need to control it. In emergency situations the Elders allow teleporting to and from restricted areas, like the Elder's room. In this case, we happened to teleport in just before Gabriel and his rescuers did. It was almost like a busy intersection with all traffic lights showing green."

"It certainly didn't improve my first teleporting experience," Sampson joked. "I think I'll stick to flying."

They all laughed, even Taylor, but then Gabriel became serious. "Sampson, I....I owe you my life, man," he said.

Sampson kept grinning. "Damn right you do. I have already started making a list of how you can reward me. You can start with no more story-telling about all the stupid stuff I've done over the years!"

Gabriel joked back: "Anything but that, please!"

"I should've left you back in prison," Sampson said. "So, are you reenergized after your little snack? I don't think you actually chewed anything."

"Yeah, it sure beat prison food, that crap was awful. I think I'm ready to speak to the Elders now."

"Forget about it," Chris said. "You need to rest for a while and let those that are older and wiser than us worry about it. They will summon you when they are ready to talk."

Gabriel yawned. "I guess I could use some sleep." He rose from his chair.

Taylor stood up, feeling awkward. "I'll, uh, walk you to your room."

Sam, Chris, and Sampson burst out laughing. "Do either of you actually know where you are going?" Sam asked.

Taylor and Gabriel looked at each other and then simultaneously shook their heads. "I'll show you," Chris said, still smiling. "We took the liberty of assigning you adjoining rooms."

After leading them to their rooms, Chris said to press triple 1 on their phones if they needed anything. Gabriel thanked him and closed the door. "Taylor, I—" he started to say.

"Shhhh, we don't need to talk about it now. I was pissed off, but now I'm not. I told you in the dream that I still love you and I do. I sort of understand why you did what you did and I know that you tried to save me in the end. You did a lot of stupid things, but I forgive you for them, which might be a mistake, but it is mine to make."

"Thank you, but….what dream?" Gabriel asked.

"You mean you didn't…? I had a dream a few days ago where you told me you loved me. I thought you had entered my dream to tell me you were okay."

Gabriel shrugged. "That would've been a good idea, but I didn't think of it and I doubt there was sufficient light in my cell to allow it. You must have dreamed me up all on your own," he said slyly.

"Don't get a big head."

"In all honesty, Tay, I thought about you every second we were apart." In one motion, Gabriel scooped her up and carried her to the bed, laying her down gently.

They held each other for hours, and although Gabriel fell asleep almost immediately, Taylor stayed awake to watch him sleep. His sleep was peaceful, his chest rising and falling with each slow, deep breath. It was probably the first good night's sleep he'd had since his capture. Taylor felt silly watching him, but she couldn't stop. She knew she shouldn't have forgiven him, shouldn't have taken him back, but her sixth sense—which she had ignored at the beginning of their relationship when it warned her about Gabriel—had changed its opinion and urged her to forgive him.

Eventually, there was a sturdy knock on the door. Taylor got up slowly, trying not to disturb Gabriel, but he stirred anyway. "What is it?" he asked.

"Someone's at the door, I think it's time to go."

Confirming her guess, Taylor found Chris, Sam, Kiren, and Sampson at the door. "It's time," Chris said.

The strange group of angels, demons, and humans quietly departed Gabriel's room. With Chris leading they made their way through the dark network of tunnels and passageways. Torches provided the only light, and the eerie glow made it feel like they were attending a séance. No one spoke as they walked, not even Sam or Sampson, the loudest ones in the bunch.

Chris and Kiren nodded to a couple of demons that passed them along the way, but didn't break stride to speak with them. Taylor gripped Gabriel's hand tightly as they followed the group, bringing up the rear. She noticed that Sam was not holding Chris's hand. It seemed that whenever Chris was in work mode, she knew better than to distract him with their feelings for each other.

Eventually, the path spilled into a small alcove. A transporter was waiting for them in silence. The glass pod looked futuristic, like something you would see in a movie or on a ride at Disneyworld.

They entered the pod. "Hang on," Chris said.

Taylor remembered Sam telling her about the last time she was in a similar transporter with Chris; he had said the exact same thing. That was a magical ride for her friend; she and Chris had just confessed their love for each other.

The doors slid shut noiselessly and the vehicle thrust forward, gaining speed with each passing second. Sampson looked impressed by the machine, likely comparing it to the hybrid elevators/transporters at angel headquarters. "Woohoo!" he yelled, as they reached maximum speed. The rocky walls whipped by on all sides. As quickly as it had accelerated, the transporter decelerated and slowed to a stop at a lonely recess carved into the tunnel.

They exited and passed through a wide open foyer that was lit by dozens of fireplaces on either side. Ignoring the demon at the security desk, Chris led them into the Elders' Chamber, where they were expected. More than 150 pairs of eyes turned to watch them enter. A table and six chairs had been set up for them.

Clifford motioned to the table and they sat down in a line, facing the Elders. Taylor felt like she was sitting at the bride and groom's table at a wedding reception. Coincidentally, she and Gabriel were placed in the direct center of the table, where the bride and groom would normally sit, flanked by Chris and Sam on the left, and Sampson and Kiren on the right.

Clearing his throat, Clifford began, "Thank you all for coming. We have a lot to be thankful for. Today we successfully completed two dangerous and challenging missions. However, in the process we lost one brave soldier, Dominique Rhodes. Let us begin with a moment of silence for our fallen brother." All heads bowed and a respectful silence ensued.

Continuing, Clifford said, "We obviously have some decisions to make regarding our future strategies in the War, but first, I would like each mission leader to brief us on their respective mission." He nodded to Sampson. "Why don't we start with the rescue mission, Operation Traitor. Sampson?" Taylor's head perked up, as she waited anxiously to hear the tale of her boyfriend's escape.

Remaining seated, Sampson said, "I'd like to start with a quick background on my involvement. Two years ago, I came to the demons in the hopes that they would take me on as a warrior in their army. I had heard a number of *things* regarding the Archangel Council's ultimate desires, nicknamed The Plan, which were strictly confidential. Needless to say, I did not like what I heard. The Elders immediately recruited me as a spy and I have been feeding them information ever since.

"When the opportunity arose to help the demon cause while also assisting an old friend in Gabriel, I was very willing to do my part." Taylor saw that Gabriel's eyes had not left his friend's face while he was speaking. He was clearly surprised at hearing how long Sampson had been spying on the angels.

Sampson then told of the planning process for the mission. "A mission of this complexity could not have been pulled off without significant resources on the inside. While, intentionally, none of the spies know who each other are, I believe there are about thirty in total?" He looked at Clifford for confirmation. The old demon nodded. Sampson continued: "And most importantly, we have one spy at the highest of levels, who arranged for us to access high-security areas, such as the prison."

Upon hearing this, Gabriel interrupted, "Are you telling me someone on the Archangel Council is working for the demons?" He looked incredulous at the mere suggestion of such insurrection.

Sampson said, "Yes." Gabriel folded his arms and leaned back in his chair, his eyebrows arched and his mouth filling with a bubble of air. What he had just learned was clearly blowing his mind. He let out the stored up breath in a long, slow blast.

Sampson then told the story of their escape. When he reached the part about Lucas's murder of the young demon, both Chris and Gabriel clenched their fists, as if they were ready to leap from their chairs and seek revenge immediately. When he finished his story, silence fell over the room.

Clifford let the information sink in for a minute before moving on. "Christopher, while you were the Operations Leader for both missions, Kiren was the Mission Leader for the retrieval of Taylor and Samantha—Operation Humanity. Kiren, why don't you take us through it."

In a very high level of detail, Kiren told the story of the car chase. By the end of her monologue, everyone was on the edge of their seats, and when she described the fire-boulder attack and the resulting destruction of the angels' high-end cars, there were a few cheers and claps amongst the audience. Kiren beamed at the response.

One demon who was not smiling was Clifford. A frown crossed his face. "That was quick-thinking and I commend you on your actions in the heat of battle, young lady, but I am more worried about a few of the key facts from your story. First, we had a spy in our midst. Adrian was assigned to this particular mission because we thought he could be trusted, but evidently we were wrong. The information that he must have fed to the angels almost single-handedly brought down the entire mission.

"Second, the angels' willingness to attack in broad daylight is particularly troubling. Our experience with them is that they are generally very cautious, but their actions bordered on reckless abandon. What do you make of it?" Clifford directed the question to the Elders, but it was Gabriel who answered.

"They will do whatever it takes to recapture Taylor." All eyes fell on Gabriel. He paused, then said, "As cocky as the angels are, they've realized that they can't defeat you guys without Taylor's help. And they let her slip through their fingers, which really pissed Dionysus off. He will be willing to take massive risks to get her back. Our only choice is to take them down first." He said the last sentence so confidently, that even Taylor thought it sounded like the right thing to do; that is, until she realized that he was volunteering to help.

"No!" she said sharply.

Gabriel turned towards Taylor, a surprised look washing over his face, as though, in the heat of the moment he had forgotten she was there. "I have to do this," he breathed.

"You'll get yourself killed," she said matter-of-factly. Continuing calmly, she said, "The way I see it, I am the key to everything." She smirked, enjoying her own joke. At least, it would have been a joke if it hadn't been true. A couple of the Elders chuckled. Sam smiled at her, evidently proud of the boldness of her friend.

Taylor continued: "So...if I am the key, then there are really only two options here. One, you kill me, or I kill myself...." Gabriel froze at her suggestion. She quickly added, "But I would prefer to not have to die, if possible. That leaves the second option: hide me away until the angels can be defeated."

Out of the corner of her eye, she saw Gabriel staring at her—his face was proud. He touched her leg under the table, but she ignored it.

One of the female Elders broke the short silence, "I think option two sounds pretty good. We protect Taylor here, until we are able to win the War. As Gabriel said, the angels will be forced to take risks to get her back and we will be waiting to exploit them."

Clifford nodded slowly. "It sounds reasonable to me, if Taylor is willing."

"I am," Taylor said.

A surprising interruption came from the end of the table. "What about school?" Sam asked. "And Taylor's father?"

"Easy," Chris said. "We can teleport into the student registry office at night, hack a few systems, and ensure her grades are good and her meal plan is used. To her dad, it will look like she is still going to school there. Anytime she needs to make an appearance, we can teleport her wherever she needs to be." He had it all figured out.

"And what about me?" Sam asked.

Chris looked down at his hands. Clifford said, "You should go back to school to help cover for Taylor. But you can come back as often as you like: after class, on the weekends, whenever you want. We will send Kiren with you, along with some other guards, to protect you." Chris leaned towards her and Taylor heard him whisper, "I'll bring you back every single night." Samantha smiled.

Clifford scanned the panel of Elders. "Does anyone have any reservations regarding this plan of attack?"

Gabriel squirmed in his seat, as silence filled the room. When no one else offered an opinion, he stood up and said, "I'm not trying to be rude, but the only decision we have made is to keep Taylor here to protect her. You just referred to it as our 'plan of attack'. It seems more like a plan of defense. What about our strategy for attacking the angels and ending the War?"

Clifford sighed. "Young angel. You see, there is the fundamental difference between our two races. Sometimes the best act is to not act at all. The Archangel Council might have been successful in destroying us already if they weren't so eager to use Taylor's power. In this case, we will wait and let Dionysus make the first move. Then, when the opportunity presents itself, we'll attack."

Gabriel looked around and saw only nodding heads. It seemed no one else in the room shared his desire to act quickly. He resigned himself to the decision that had been made and, reluctantly, sat down.

"If no one else has anything to discuss, I adjourn this meeting and will leave it to Chris, as the Operations Leader, to make any necessary arrangements." With that, Clifford and the other Elders began disappearing in bunches from the room—apparently the teleporting rules did not apply to them.

The six at the long table arose slowly and wordlessly. As they passed through the foyer and back onto the transporter, Sam asked, "What should we do now?"

"Let's just enjoy the holidays," Chris said with a smile.

Ten

Taylor awoke and sighed with satisfaction. She felt warm. She felt loved. Complete even. Her arm was draped across Gabriel's bare chest. She could feel his pectoral muscles flex gently each time his lungs filled with air.

Ever so gradually, she lifted her arm from across him, making a conscious effort not to wake her sleeping boyfriend. Just when she thought she was successful, Gabriel's eyes shot open, his strong arms pulling her back onto him. Taylor laughed in surprise as he kissed her face, her neck. When he reached her lips, he lingered for what could have been an eternity, or just a few seconds—Taylor couldn't tell which.

Taylor had forgiven Gabriel for all of his lies, for his treachery, even for putting her own life in danger. He had paid for his sins while in prison, by nearly losing his own life. But she did have one requirement of him, which he had readily agreed to. "Come on," Taylor said, pulling her lips away from his. "It's story day."

Gabriel cringed. "Maybe we should just wait until after the holidays, then I will tell you everything."

"You promised," Taylor said. "You owe it to me."

"Okay, you're right. Today is story day."

"*True* story day," Taylor reminded him.

"Right."

Ever since Taylor's discovery that Gabriel had woven lies into his story about the evolution of angels and demons, she had been itching to hear him tell the true story. Chris offered to tell her, but she refused—she wanted to hear it from Gabriel.

It was the 30th of December, and Taylor wanted to hear the story before she became distracted with the New Year's celebrations that the demons were planning. According to Chris, despite being nonhuman, they really knew how to throw a party.

Taylor had showered the night before, so she got ready quickly—she never did her hair or used makeup—and waited patiently for Gabriel to shower and dress. Despite her efforts, Taylor and Gabriel were the last ones to arrive at breakfast. Chris and Sam had already finished, while Sampson and Kiren had apparently just arrived too, and were only beginning to eat.

Taylor filled her plate; the demon cafe was set up similar to the college dining hall: buffet-style with various options scattered throughout the café. Within minutes she was finished eating, while Gabriel was taking his sweet, old time—he must have been chewing each bite at least thirty times.

The second that the last forkful of sausage hit his tongue, Taylor said, "Okay, who's ready for story time?"

Surprisingly, the first to answer was Kiren. "I am definitely in. When else will I get the opportunity to listen to an angel tell the dark truth about his people?"

"Hey!" Sampson objected. "I've been helping the Elders out for years."

"Oh, sorry, Sampson. I wasn't counting you as one of *them*."

"And I am?" Gabriel asked.

"You're still a recovering angel as far as I'm concerned," she replied. "You have to make it through the 12-step program before I will fully believe you."

"What are the steps?" Taylor asked.

"Well, step one is what he is about to do." Kiren motioned to Gabriel. "Admit he was wrong, that he lied, that most angels are evil, that sort of thing. I'll tell you the rest of the steps later. We don't want to overwhelm him just yet."

"Good luck, buddy," Sampson said, slapping his friend on the back. "You should have taken the easy route like I did, and just become a spy."

Gabriel smirked. "Thanks for the advice." Looking at Kiren, he added, "And don't you worry. I am going to show you that I am committed to helping you take down the Archangel Council and anyone who supports them."

"Okay, then let's start with step one, angel-boy," Taylor said.

"I've got the perfect spot," Chris said, winking at Taylor.

As they walked, Chris spouted off facts about the Lair.

The Lair was comprised of a labyrinth of tunnels, alcoves, caves and cisterns. The massive underground network covered five square miles, including escape access tunnels and natural resource reserves. In typical demon style, there was very little rhyme and even less reason to the floor plan. Rather, over the years additions were made as random offshoots from the original underground structure.

In its infancy, the Lair was simple, with only an eating area, a sleeping area (which was a large, domed room), and a meeting area. Over the last hundred years, it had been expanded to include 5,000 separate, hotel-style rooms, more than 200 transporters—allowing residents and guests to access any part of the complex in mere minutes—a recreational room (used heavily by Taylor and Sam, mostly for its pool tables), and other luxuries meant to improve the overall standard of living.

They passed through a thick metal door and down a long, curving path. Taylor casually ran her hand along the stone wall as she walked. In this particular passageway, the stone walls were perfectly smooth, in direct contrast to the rough rock walls in most other areas of the Lair. Eventually they reached a break in the wall, as the tunnel tapered off to form a large alcove. Within the recess, it was well-lit, with more than a dozen amply-burning torches secured to the walls.

"What is this place?" Taylor asked.

"You'll see," Chris responded furtively. There was a gleam in his eyes.

At the far end of the space were four sets of wrought-iron double doors, lined up like soldiers on the front lines. None were open.

Chris approached one of them. Before he opened it, Taylor spotted faint lettering on the outside that read: "To Balcony".

He pulled the door open and then held it for the tour group behind him. They marched through in a single-file formation, the door being only wide enough for a single body to pass through at a time.

At the front of the pack, Taylor plunged into darkness, waving her hands in front of her, as the bright foyer transitioned into a narrow strait—it was pitch black. A light flicked on from behind her, and the path before her was suddenly bathed in a white sheen. She glanced back over her shoulder.

"Flashlight. An angel's best friend," Gabriel explained. While his favorite Mag-lite flashlight had been confiscated by the angels during his arrest and imprisonment, Sampson was able to procure another one for him before busting him out of prison. Gabriel prodded Taylor gently in the small of her back with his hand, encouraging her to continue forward.

Resuming her march, Taylor reached a steep staircase. As there were no handrails, she steadied her climb by running her hands along the walls, which were now not only smooth, but cold. *Marble*, she thought. That explained the sheen when the flashlight was illuminated. Someone went to a lot of trouble to add a touch of elegance to this place. She knew it must be a special place to the demons.

When she had climbed the final step, she heard Chris yell from below, "Wait for me when you get to the top, Taylor!" Obediently, she took a couple of steps forward to allow the others enough room to exit the stairs, and then waited for Christopher. Thirty seconds later, Chris had squeezed past the group and was standing on her right. On her other side, Gabriel probed his flashlight around them. Regardless of which direction he aimed it, the light disappeared into darkness, unable to find a wall or ceiling to rest upon. The room must be huge. As he played the beam along the ground, it uncovered what appeared to be clusters of stone benches arranged in semi-circles; each cluster also had a circle of smaller stones in the midst of them—they looked like fire pits at a camp site.

Taylor repeated her previous question. "What is this place?"

She could barely make out Chris's smile under the glow of Gabriel's body. "You're about to find out." He dramatically stretched his arm out in front of him and paused. When he snapped his fingers a small flame appeared, like his finger was a lighter. The flame slowly grew into a small fire and then, using both hands like he was shaping dough to make Christmas cookies, he formed a ball of fire. Taylor and Sam leaned closer, in awe of the way his skin refused to burn. While the demons' mastery of fire was something that Chris, Kiren, Gabriel and Sampson had grown up with, the spectacle was still fresh and new to the human girls.

Chris grinned, enjoying the attention. Rapidly, he whipped his arm back and kicked his leg high in the air, like a Major League pitcher preparing to throw a fast ball, and then thrust his arm forward. The fireball shot from his palm and tore through the gloom. After twenty yards, the flaming sphere's flight ended abruptly, as it collided with an unseen object in their direct line of sight. An explosion of fire and flame erupted upwards, spreading rapidly. *Something wasn't right,* Taylor thought, as the flames branched further outwards, extending their domain. *He was going to burn the place down!*

Sam read her mind. "Chris, we gotta get out of here," she shouted, grabbing his shoulder.

He looked back, surprised at the reaction. "I wanted to surprise you, but perhaps I should have given you some warning. It's fine. Just watch."

The girls looked on, their fear slowly morphing into excitement, as the initial cylinder of fire spread along the curved atrium roof, creating a dozen concentric circles linked by fiery spokes. Each burning circle was of a larger diameter than the previous one and, when the final circle had formed, four plumes of fire blazed from the base of the domed roof. As if by magic, hundreds of tiny torches and lanterns were lit throughout the dome, shedding light on the furthest reaches of the space.

Looking back at where Chris's fireball had originally ignited the fire, Taylor could see that the raging inferno was, in actuality, a fiery chandelier, as beautiful as it was deadly. She stepped forward to a curved railing and looked down. They were on a large balcony, as the sign on the door had suggested, and below them were hundreds more of the stone seating areas. Beyond the lower-level seats was a massive slab of smooth, round rock. It appeared to be a stage.

"Is this a theater?" Taylor asked.

Still grinning, Chris said, "Yep. Welcome to Demon Hall, where all the popular acts by the Demon Symphony and the Demon Play Company have been held over the last hundred years. We have also had a number of great shows by some of the best demon rocks bands, too," he added.

Sam and Taylor looked at him like he was mad, but he just shrugged and said, "Saving humans from complete destruction by the angel race is not exactly a full-time job. There's lots of down time and we need to entertain ourselves somehow. I'm sure the angels have the same thing, right, Gabriel?"

Sampson and Gabriel looked at each other and laughed. Gabriel said, "Actually, no. We do play games and eat and talk and have fun, but I can say with certainty that we have nothing like this. I am pretty impressed."

Chris's smile widened and it was evident that Kiren was doing her best not to laugh out loud at the thought of one-upping the angels. While the girls continued to gaze around the Hall in awe, Chris said, "Anyway, I thought it would be a nice location for story time, don't you think?"

"Absolutely. Thanks, Chris," Sam said, hugging her boyfriend proudly.

"Yeah, thanks," Taylor agreed.

Walking arm in arm with Samantha, Chris led them to one of the nearby stone clusters. Each bench looked like a miniature Stonehenge, with two rocks on either end, supporting a long, rectangular stone that served as a seat for four or five people...or demons...or angels, at a time.

The only two without significant others, Sampson sat with Gabriel and Taylor, and Kiren sat with Christopher and Samantha. Gabriel clicked off his flashlight, which was rendered useless by Chris's powerful fire display. Chris ignited another small flame on his finger and lit the small fire pit in the center of the seating area.

"What do we do next, sing 'Kumbayah' and roast marshmallows?" Sampson asked.

Chuckling, Chris retorted, "We will be branding your butt with the demon insignia, so you always remember which side you are on."

"You can do both of my cheeks if you want, since I've caused so many problems," Gabriel suggested.

"Aww, man, no one wants to see that!" Sampson joked.

"I might," Taylor said. "Remember, this whole trip is all about causing angel-boy as much pain as possible. Just getting him to tell this story has been like getting a child to take a bath."

Gabriel smirked. "Alright, alright. I get the hint. I will tell you the entire truth as I know it...from the beginning. Chris, Kiren—I would ask that you interrupt if anything I say is different from your understanding. I want to get this right." The two demons nodded seriously.

Under the mood-setting flicker of firelight, with Taylor's hand intertwined with his, Gabriel began the tale that he had once told Taylor—it seemed like a lifetime ago, but was, in reality, only a few months earlier. The tale began exactly as Taylor knew it from before: Clifford Dempsey the explorer, the snake bite, the *changes* Clifford underwent, and his subsequent astonishment over his newfound powers. Clifford was the beginning of the demon evolution.

When Gabriel reached the part about Clifford being called *daemon* by the woman and being shunned by the villagers, Taylor noticed a change in the tone of his voice. In his previous story, he had made Clifford sound angry, as he described the darkness that clouded his mind, the evil that crept into his soul. But this time around, Gabriel described Clifford as distraught; he wept for many hours. He had never felt so alone in his life—he was a freak, hated by all, never to be accepted into society again.

Clifford lay in the forest for days, under the cover of the trees—not eating, not drinking, not sleeping. Soaked with his own tears, he began to hate what he had become. Eventually, a single beam of light navigated its way through the dense web of branches and leaves, and found its way through Clifford's shroud of darkness to his face. Feeling the warmth on his cheeks, he suddenly felt alive, invigorated, and most importantly, full of hope.

He sprang to his feet and found a spot where the sun shone brightly—a clearing. Soaking up the life-giving rays, he began to practice with his new powers. Within days he had mastered his power over fire, and soon after, his ability to control the weather. Finally, he learned to temporarily cast off the dark shroud that plagued him. Weeping with joy, Clifford began planning his reentry into society.

Taylor was shocked to learn that the remainder of the story was completely different than what he had told her originally. The breadth of the lies that Gabriel had so easily poured into her head was appalling. Her chest began to tighten and her breathing became shallow.

She released the grip of her fingers, one by one, until she could pull her hand free from his. She folded her hands together, took a deep breath, and continued to listen. Gabriel glanced at her, but then continued on with the story.

Gabriel told them how Clifford had, in fact, repatriated into society. But not as an outlaw, as Gabriel had tricked Taylor into believing, but as a deputy sheriff in a small town. Clifford soon made his mark by displaying extraordinary feats of bravery, as he quickly eradicated all crime from the town. The sheriff offered to step down, to let Clifford take on his position, but he declined, happy just to be a part of something good.

As his reputation grew, Clifford became the most desirable bachelor in town, but many of the women that pursued him seemed crass, and only wanted him for his fame. He waited patiently, politely declining all invitations until one day when he was watering his horse, a young woman rode up. As she dismounted her steed, their eyes locked and Clifford's heart swooned. She was the most beautiful woman he had ever laid eyes on. With deep, brown eyes and ash-blond hair, the warmth and depth of her character pierced his heart, even before she had spoken one word to him. Clifford knew this was the woman he would marry.

Soon he discovered that she was working her way west, in search of a fresh start. Her husband and two children had been killed by a murderous gang of outlaws. While Clifford could not fully cure the sadness in her eyes, he vowed to always protect her. Her name was Adele Montrose. Within weeks they had married and she was pregnant with their first child together.

Clifford kept his secret from her until after their child was born—a son. Immediately, Clifford knew that the boy wasn't fully human. A layer of darkness surrounded him like a blanket. Pouring out his soul to Adele, he told her everything: what he was, what he was capable of, and that their son was probably the same. At the end of his tale, Clifford hung his head in shame, waiting for her to run from him screaming, like the native woman in the Amazon.

The next thing he felt was the warmth of a kiss on his forehead, an arm around him, and a gentle voice. "If you are a demon, then I hope my son is a demon, too," she said. Clifford's heart filled with joy as his eyes met hers. He held her tight for many hours that night.

Over the next thirty years, Clifford and Adele bore many children. Each of them had Clifford's curse—or gift, as Adele called it. He taught them to use their powers, and to use them for good. The family business was protecting innocent people, and the Dempsey's were good at what they did. Soon he was a grandfather, and his family enjoyed many years of prosperity. But it couldn't last.

Four generations later in 1950, long after Clifford and Adele had died, a demon child was born, Dionysus was his name. He was brought up just like the other demon children, taught to protect humans, to share the world with them. But for some reason, it didn't take. His thoughts were filled with grand plans and dreams of power.

By the time Dionysus was eighteen he had become destructive, committing heinous acts of crime against humans. Some of his violence had spilled into the family. When confronted by his father, he scoffed at him, telling him that he was weak and small-minded. His father's name was Clifford.

Eleven

Taylor's head jolted up. "What?" she said.

Gabriel didn't answer. Instead, he waited for her to process what he had just said. Taylor looked at Christopher, at Kiren, at Sampson. No one objected to Gabriel's statement. It must be true. "The head of the demon Elders is Dionysus's father," she said. It wasn't a question. She understood.

Instinctively, she reached for Gabriel's hand and clutched it tightly. She felt the warmth of his touch trickle up her arm and then, like a waterfall, pour through her entire body. Her initial anger at realizing the extent of his lies gave way to forgiveness, and she found herself crying, not tears of fear, or of sadness, or of pain, but rather, tears of understanding. Gabriel had grown up in an environment that was engineered by a madman—a mad-angel—who sought to brainwash innocent children into carrying out his sadistic plans.

Composing herself, Taylor wiped the tears away with the back of her hand, her face flushing in embarrassment. She hoped the light of the fire wasn't sufficient to illuminate her warm cheeks. She hated crying. She said, "You didn't grow up knowing the truth, right?"

Sampson spoke for the first time. "As kids, we were taught the story that Gabriel told you the first time. That demons were evil; that angels were the protectors of humans. Dionysus was the first angel so he was able to make things up as he went along."

Taylor nodded. "Please continue," she urged Gabriel.

Looking hesitant, he put his arm around her and spoke slowly. "The angel evolution occurred exactly as I told you before. Dionysus forced the demon darkness off of him and painstakingly pieced himself back together using the power of the sun. The result was the creation of a new race, one that would become an instant enemy to the demons. Naturally, he took on the name of *angel*."

But Gabriel didn't stop there. With each word, he looked like he was casting off a great burden, one that had tormented him for some time. The truth really was setting him free, and he wasn't about to stop until he had spilled his guts.

He laid out, in intricate detail, The Plan that had been formulated by Dionysus and the Archangel Council. The Plan was to destroy the demons—who were protecting the humans—and then enslave humankind. Not to be used as pets or as labor, the humans would be used by the angels to release the bounds of mortality. By extracting the aura of a human, Gabriel explained, and replacing it with an angel's inner light, the angel could take on the body of the human while still maintaining their angel abilities. Thus, angels could live forever.

When Gabriel explained The Plan, Taylor, Samantha, Sampson, Kiren, and even Christopher leaned in, hanging on every word. None of them had been privy to the full extent of the information. If the demon Elders were aware of The Plan, they had kept it secret from the demon army. When Gabriel stopped speaking, the room fell silent as each of them stared into the fire, lost in their own thoughts.

As usual, Samantha broke the silence. "What a bunch of sicko's," she said.

"I thought it was bad enough that the angels were trying to destroy the human race," Chris said, "but this is far more evil."

Sampson said, "When did you find out about this, Gabriel?" His tone was accusing.

Knowing she was the only one who could stop the verbal assault that was sure to come, Taylor said, "He found out about it before he came to kidnap me. He made a major, serious, worst-possible, disgusting mistake, but he has shown that he is ready to atone for that mistake. He has proven that by coming here today, by admitting to his lies, and he is about to vow to stop Dionysus, no matter what it takes." Taylor looked expectantly at Gabriel.

He looked at her, confused for a moment, and then realized what she was waiting for. "Oh, yes, of course. I vow to help the demons in their quest to stop Dionysus," he said solemnly.

"No matter what it takes," Taylor reminded.

"No matter what it takes."

Taylor looked into the eyes of each demon, her best friend, and the remaining angel, and said, "If it's good enough for me—and it is—then it needs to be good enough for you. Given that I have been hurt the most from all of this, my forgiveness should be enough."

They each nodded once, although Sampson continued to glare at Gabriel.

Twelve

At first the group walked in silence, moving reverently back down the stairs and out into the passageway, but before long Samantha had them all talking and laughing again. She was telling them a story about her last New Year's Eve experience.

"My dad tried to set off fireworks in the backyard. He had bought them illegally in Mexico—he thought he would impress me and my mom by being a rebel—but when he lit the fuse, it kept burning out. So finally, he tried to light the M-80 directly, where the fuse meets the firework, and something went wrong and it didn't light right. It began spinning and shooting off sparks everywhere. My dad started dancing around like he was walking on hot sand or something. That's when his shorts caught on fire. My mom ran over and pushed him to the ground and he rolled around until the fire went out. Stop, drop, and roll really worked for him. All that was left of his shorts were a few charred pieces of tattered denim, and underneath he was wearing glow in the dark Valentine's Day boxer shorts that my mom had bought him a few years earlier. It was one of the funniest, most disturbing things I have ever seen."

By the time she got to the "stop, drop and roll" part, everyone was laughing loudly. Even Sampson's anger subsided, making way for his contagious smile.

"Well, I doubt we'll witness anything that funny this year," Chris said, "but I can promise you it will be entertaining. The Demon Spectacular has gotten bigger and bigger each year. I've heard rumors that even the angels watch it from the safety of their mountain."

"It's true," Sampson confirmed. "You're in for a treat."

"Excellent," Taylor said. "I think we can all use something to take our mind off of reality."

They spent the rest of the day hanging out and talking, but mostly they were laughing. Sampson was back to his old self and was telling stories of the trouble that he and Gabriel used to get into as kids. They played a few games of pool, relaxed on the massive couches in the recreation room, and ate until they could eat no more. It felt like they were back at college— before everything had happened. For the next few days, at least, they all hoped that life would be good again.

The calm wouldn't last as long as they hoped.

PART II

"I can't remember anything
Can't tell if this is true or dream
Deep down inside I feel the scream
This terrible silence stops it there

Now that the war is through with me
I'm waking up, I cannot see
That there's not much left of me
Nothing is real but pain now

Hold my breath as I wish for death
Oh please God, help me"

Metallica- "One"
From the album *And Justice For All (1989)*

Thirteen

It was New Year's Eve. Gabriel and Taylor had spent the entire day together, alone with just each other as company. Now that he had purged himself of his lies, and Taylor had been able to forgive him, he felt clean again. Pure, somehow. While their relationship felt deeper and more meaningful, it had also gone full circle, back to a time when all they needed was a sunny day and each other to be happy. It was an easy kind of love. Carefree.

Chris had given them directions to a cliff on the mountainside that would provide them with privacy and the chance to get some fresh air. They eagerly took him up on the offer and had spent the day sunning themselves—

sometimes talking, sometimes not. There was never an awkward silence; even silence was comfortable, beautiful.

※

Grudgingly gathering up the blanket and bag, while wishing they could stay for a few more hours, Taylor wondered what Sampson wanted to talk to Gabriel about. The only reason they couldn't stay longer was that Sampson had asked Gabriel if he could speak with him in private before the New Year's celebration. What could he want? *No need to worry*, she thought, Gabriel would gladly share their conversation with her afterwards. He had vowed never to keep anything from her again. And to her surprise, she believed him. She hoped she wasn't making another stupid mistake.

After making their way down more than a thousand steps, Gabriel kissed her goodbye. As usual, the kiss left her drunk with passion. It was not your typical goodbye peck on the lips. It was more of a I'm-never-going-to-see-you-again-because-I'm-off-to-war kind of kiss. This didn't worry her though, because he always kissed like that. Good morning kisses, nice to see you kisses, just for the hell of it kisses, and especially goodnight kisses: they were always full of passion. Even though Taylor wasn't the romantic type, she had to hand it to him: he was very consistent in the kiss department.

Staggering slightly, Taylor went in search of Sam, to occupy herself until Gabriel returned. Gabriel headed in the other direction.

ʂʑ

The passageways were extremely crowded, as off-duty demons, many of whom were involved in the evening's festivities, prepared for the big event. Gabriel had promised to meet Sampson in Demon Hall. Chris had verified that it would be empty and they would be free to talk in private there.

Echoing Taylor's question, Gabriel wondered what his best friend from birth wanted to talk to him about. A good guess was that he would want to talk about why Gabriel had been willing to help out the Council even after he knew the truth. Gabriel thought about possible responses. Temporary insanity maybe. Or blind ambition. Neither answer would satisfy Sampson. Another side of his brain clung to hope that maybe Sampson just wanted to talk strategy. You know, make sure the two angels were on the same page before the Elders started making any plans. Probably not.

Arriving at the alcove, he made his way through the *To Balcony* door, and bounded up the stairs using his Maglite to guide him. Sampson was waiting.

"Thanks for coming," he said evenly.

"Listen, Sampson, before you start, can I just say that I was a fool and was blinded by my ambition, by a miserable, pointless desire to get ahead in life. I have completely realized the idiocy of my choices and have truly vowed to make amends for them. Lastly, I am so sorry that I was ever dishonest with you and didn't tell you what I knew. Of all people, I should have told you." He finished his soliloquy with a gasp—he had forgotten to breathe while the words rushed out.

To his surprise, Sampson laughed loudly at his friend. "You thought I asked you to come here to yell at you? I forgave you within a half-hour, man. I know that the angel that did all those stupid things is not who you really are."

Gabriel looked at him blankly. "Okay, you got me then. What did you want to talk about?"

"While you've been out romancing your girl, I've been plugged into the ongoing situation. It's time for you to get back involved, man."

"I am involved. I didn't realize there was an 'ongoing situation'. I thought we were just supposed to play it cool for now."

"That just means we aren't going to attack the angels in their stronghold anytime soon, but it doesn't mean there isn't any activity happening. The Elders decided to let you have a few days to rest and reunite with Taylor before bringing you back into the strategy sessions. They asked me to talk to you now."

Gabriel's face contorted with anger. "You mean you've been involved in strategy sessions and I haven't? And you didn't tell me? What is that all about, man?" His voice took on an accusatory tone.

His words oozing with sarcasm, Sampson replied, "Yeah, we never keep anything from each other, huh, Gabriel?"

Gabriel's head dropped, as he remembered that he was in no position to lay blame on anyone. "I'm...I'm sorry, man. You're right. But why did you keep it from me?"

"I agreed with the Elders. You needed some time to recharge, both physically and mentally. Did you not enjoy your day with Taylor today?"

"Actually, it was awesome. I really needed it."

"You're welcome. I was in strategy sessions all day. We designed eight or nine plans, each of which ended in the garbage can. It was a big waste of time." Sampson looked stressed, his brow furrowed in concern. "It's all my fault."

"Plans for what?" Gabriel asked. "And what's your fault?"

"We have a bit of a situation, which is what I wanted to talk to you about."

"What kind of a situation?"

"The kind where a lot of good friends die," Sampson said cryptically.

Gabriel waited for his friend to iron out his thoughts. He could tell that he was going through a rough patch. Typically, Sampson was as sure of himself as anyone that Gabriel knew. He made decisions quickly and they always turned out to be the right ones. He was confident, but not cocky. Everyone liked him. After a minute of silence, Gabriel said, "Man, you've been my best friend for a long time and I am not going to leave you hanging. Whatever this is, we're going to work it out together."

Sampson looked at him with pained eyes. "All of the other angel spies are going to die because of me."

Oh crap, Gabriel thought. He had completely forgotten about the other angel spies—the ones who had helped him to escape. Hadn't the plan been for them to get out of angel headquarters as soon as possible after the prison break? "Where are they?" Gabriel asked.

"As far as we know, they're still inside that hell-hole. Probably in prison, awaiting execution. They went dark yesterday. At first we were still receiving reports that everything seemed to be fine, that the angels were pissed that you had escaped, but that they were merely back to planning for the next battle. That's when all communications stopped. For all we know, they could be dead already."

Gabriel's heart sank. "Sampson, this is not your fault. If it's anyone's, it's mine. They risked their lives to break me out."

"At least they chose to try to help you. They didn't have a choice on how the rescue mission would be carried out. I helped the demons design it. One of the key decisions was that the remaining angel spies would stay on the inside, so that we could continue to gather intel. They should have escaped when we did. Now they're dead."

Gabriel had never heard Sampson sound so pessimistic. "We don't know that. The angels probably just increased security and now sending out messages is too difficult. It's not like we can just fly back in and check that they're okay. I think we need to be patient."

"That's the same conclusion we came to today after hours of designing—and shooting holes through—various plans. There's a battle scheduled for tomorrow, the first battle of the new year, and our hope is that the angel spies will be on the battlefield and we can rescue them then."

"I think that's a smart plan. I will help you find them and get them to safety. I promise you." The look of determination in Gabriel's eyes seemed to encourage Sampson. The defeated look in his eyes lifted, and a steely resolve replaced it.

"Thanks, man. We'll do it together."

They embraced, pounding each other's backs firmly.

Fourteen

While Gabriel and Sampson were having their private conversation, Taylor was able to track down Samantha. Not surprisingly, she was wasting the day away at a pool table with Chris and Kiren. The recreational room was crowded with dozens of demons enjoying their holidays. The room was dark, as the shadowy beings cloaked most of the light provided by the fiery wall-fixtures. She squirmed her way through the crowd and over to her friends, who occupied a corner table. When Taylor arrived, her friends were playing *Cut-throat*, a three-person game where each player tries to pocket the other players' balls. At the moment, Sam and Kiren were ganging up on Chris, who was a far superior player, to try to eliminate his last ball, the green six-ball.

"The two-ball is a much easier shot," he was saying when Taylor walked in.

"Yeah, but the six-ball is yours, and Kiren and I have made a temporary truce," Sam replied. There was a *choo* sound, followed by a soft clink when the white cue-ball contacted the six-ball. From across the room, Taylor heard a soft *thump* as one of the balls fell into the corner pocket.

"Yes!!" Sam exclaimed. Apparently the six-ball had been eliminated.

Chris groaned. "I guess I can't win them all," he said, embracing Sam. "Nice shot, babe." He kissed her hard on the lips.

Kiren looked away and saw Taylor approaching. "Thank God," she said. "Ever since Sampson left, I have been stuck here as the third wheel and these two can't seem to keep their hands off of each other."

Taylor grinned. "I know what you mean, but I can't really talk, Gabriel and I are pretty bad, too."

Upon hearing Taylor's voice, Sam and Chris ended their public display of affection. "Hey, Tay," Sam said. Then, turning to Kiren, she said, "You can't talk either, Kiren, you were getting pretty flirty with Mr. Sampson during that second game of pool." She grinned slyly.

Kiren blushed. Or at least that's what Taylor thought it looked like. Her face just got a bit darker—a demon blush. She denied it. "I don't know what you're talking about, we were just having a little fun. I don't care which side he's on—he's still an angel."

Sam shrugged, turning back to Taylor. "How was your romantic day with Gabriel?"

"Perfect, thanks, guys. We both really needed it."

"No problem," Chris said from across the table. "Up for a game of pool while you wait for him to come back? Kiren could use a teammate."

"Sure, but don't you want to finish your game first?"

"Well, Sam just knocked me out of the game, so it's up to her and Kiren."

"I forfeit," Kiren said flatly. "Watching Chris lose was good enough for me. I prefer doubles." She sounded like she was talking about tennis.

The game commenced with Taylor and Kiren at a distinct disadvantage given that the best player was on the other team. Taylor was shocked at how much better Sam had gotten, too. *She must have been playing all day*, Taylor thought. In less than five minutes the game was over, with Chris sinking the eight-ball using a pretty bank shot into the center pocket. Taylor and Kiren still had four striped balls on the table.

"Rematch?" Sam asked smugly.

Taylor was saved from having to chicken out when Gabriel reappeared just then. Sampson was close behind him. At the sight of her boyfriend, Taylor smiled widely. His lips curled into a grin, but she could tell that it was forced. Something had chilled his happy mood considerably. Something Sampson said. Or something Sampson did. Wanting to know what their secret conversation was about, she was about to suggest to Gabriel that they get some food to go and eat back in their rooms, when Sampson said, "Gabriel and I would like to talk to everyone about something."

Chris started to say, "I'm not sure now is the right time—" but Sampson cut him off.

"The Elders asked me to tell everyone, after telling Gabriel first."

Sampson got right to the point. "The angel spies have not communicated with us since early yesterday. We are assuming they have been discovered and will be executed as traitors. Given the last prisoner's miraculous escape," he looked at Gabriel with a smirk, "we suspect they may act much quicker this time around."

"What can we do?" Sam asked.

"Nothing. We just want everyone to know what the situation is and that we may have to act quickly to save them if necessary," Gabriel said.

"What do you mean by 'we'? Who will have to act to save them?" Taylor asked.

Sampson fielded her question: "We have created a special task force for the mission. It will be comprised of me, Kiren, Chris, Gabriel, and some of the other highly trained demons that helped to bust Gabriel out."

Taylor wanted to object. Everything in her heart urged her, even commanded her to cry out, to say, "No! He can't leave me again, I've just found him!" But she knew her cries would be fruitless. He would feel responsible for the lives of those angels and nothing she could say would stop him from leaving if he was needed. She searched the eyes of each person in the circle and, on most of them, she saw determination and resolve, but when she reached Sam's face, it was like looking in a mirror. Fear was all she saw. Fear of losing her true love. Fear of being alone again. Fear of never feeling safe. They were sisters in fear. At least for now.

Fifteen

The close group of friends, which now included Kiren and Sampson, who were quickly becoming core members of the group, had dinner and then each went back to their rooms to rest before the festivities that were planned for the evening. While the news from Sampson had come as a shock and had put a bit of a damper on the day, they were still excited about enjoying an evening of entertainment, a chance to escape from the worries of real life.

Chris had locked in the best seat in the house—the same spot where he had picnicked with Sam just before the fateful battle where Gabriel was taken prisoner. It was also the cliff cave where, on Chris's suggestion, Taylor and

Gabriel had spent the day. A few of the Elders, including Clifford, would be joining them to watch the show.

At eight o'clock in the evening, in near synchronization, the six friends emerged from their rooms and spilled into the residential hallway. Despite the fact that they were in a massive cave network, Taylor had already grown so accustomed to the fire-lit passageways that the place felt somewhat homey to her. She had begun referring to the room as her bedroom, and to the passageways as hallways.

Reaching the right doorway, they began the thousand-step ascent to the familiar cliff cave.

Taylor's thoughts were muddled. While she wanted to relax and just enjoy the celebration, her mind wandered back to her fears. At any moment, Gabriel could be called upon to execute a mission that he may never come back from. *Screw that*, Taylor thought. She wasn't about to sit idly by and watch him get killed. Earlier that day, she had made plans of her own.

While the others had been resting, Taylor had knocked on Samantha's door. For two hours the girls talked about the men in their lives. Not like some gossipy, complaining girls' night out, nor like obsessed, love-crazed teenagers. Rather, they spoke about soul mates, about how life without Gabriel and Christopher would be like life without air, or water; and mostly, they spoke about how they could help them. Save them even. They plotted and schemed, and by the end of the conversation they had concocted a variety of plans that could be used in various circumstances.

Their plans were reckless—that much they admitted to themselves—but these were reckless times. Throwing caution to the wind may put their own lives in jeopardy, but it might also be the only way to save them from a life not lived—a life without love.

Although Taylor felt better after talking to her best friend—she now felt like she was actually doing something, rather than just waiting around—she could still not shake the ominous feeling of foreboding that crept into her heart, filling her with fear. As she felt Gabriel's hand on her lower back, she tried to focus on his touch and the love that resonated from it. She wanted to look into his eyes, but she was afraid that it would give away her intentions. That somehow he would know what she had been planning. She laughed at her own paranoia. While he had many powers, mind reading was *not* one of them.

"What is it? What's so funny?" he asked her.

Surprised by his question, Taylor realized that she had actually laughed out loud at her own thoughts. "Uh, nothing. I was just thinking about how Sam beat Chris at pool earlier," she lied smoothly.

"Really? When was that?"

"When you were talking to Sampson. She was quite proud of herself."

"As she should be, that's impressive."

They continued on in silence, listening to Sam chatter away with Chris. She was asking him a million questions a minute about what to expect from the evening: how long the show was, the history of it, who created it, how many demons were involved in its production, and on and on. Happy for a distraction from her thoughts, Taylor listened as Chris explained that the Demon Spectacular was first created in 1982 when Wooster Child, an engineer in the demon army, complained that the troops needed something to take their minds off of the War, especially during the holidays. Liking the idea, the Elders provided Wooster with a small budget and allowed him to ask for volunteers to help with the show. The response was overwhelming; so many demons signed up that he didn't know what to do with them all. He enlisted the help of five of his closest friends, who became co-directors. Their first show was a huge success, and each subsequent year the budget was expanded and the planning began earlier and earlier in the year.

Now, twenty years later, the production included over 500 demons, including the cast and crew, and commanded a budget of $10 million. Mr. Child remained as the overall director, relishing his role and the challenge of surprising his viewers with something new in each show. Demons from all over the world teleported to the Lair on New Year's Eve each year, as the Lair's population soared from 5,000 to over 20,000.

Reaching the summit, they flowed into the small cave. There were half a dozen demons already gathered on the cliff's edge, peering out into the night sky. Hearing voices, they turned to greet the new arrivals. Before she could make out his face, Taylor recognized his voice. "Welcome, friends," Clifford said.

"Thank you, sir," Chris replied. "And thanks for inviting us to join you for the entertainment."

"Ahh, my pleasure, my dear boy. I wanted our guests to have the opportunity to view this year's installment of the Demon Spectacular in its full glory."

"Thanks, Cliff," Samantha replied casually.

Smiling, Clifford spoke directly to Samantha, "Come, my dear, you can sit next to me." He led her to a blanket where they sat next to each other cross-legged. Chris followed her, sitting on her other side. Taylor, Gabriel, Kiren and Sampson found similar seats on empty blankets that had been laid out for them. There were five others already seated on the cliff. Taylor thought she recognized their faces from the panel of Elders earlier that week.

"Would you like me to tell you about the history of the Spectacular?" Clifford asked. His question wasn't directed at anyone in particular, but he turned towards Samantha for a response.

Despite having just heard the same information from Chris, Sam said, "Sure. Thanks, Cliff. That would be great."

While Clifford went into a much more detailed chronicle of the Demon Spectacular from its inception, Taylor held Gabriel's hand tightly and watched as a buzz of activity filled the valley below. From high above, the demons appeared to scurry like ants in search of food, their movements seemingly random, without pattern. Flaming torches had been set up throughout the valley, providing them with a low level of light while they worked.

Taylor inched forward and craned her neck to get a better view of the mountain below her. She could make out hundreds, maybe thousands, of shadowy forms that were only visible because of the moonlight. They were scattered along the side of the mountain. All waiting, waiting.

A single flare shot high into the air. Clifford paused in his monologue, and said, "Ahh, yes. It's starting!" The bright orb travelled higher and higher, until Taylor thought it might break through the atmosphere and into outer space, never to be seen again. Just when she thought it was headed for the moon, the flare reached its peak and stopped, defying gravity as it hung in the air. Its light went out, fizzling away like it had never been.

Taylor whispered, "What happened?"

Having seen the Spectacular many times from the other side of the valley, Gabriel replied softly, "Just wait."

A minute passed in silence, then two. When she was nearly bored from the anticipation, the dark firmament suddenly erupted in flame. Reds, oranges, and yellows filled her view, bursting in every direction. Balls of fire arced across the sky, and then exploded in midair, never reaching the ground. It was as if the gates of Hell had been opened and all of the Devil's weapons were being used simultaneously. That, or one of the mountains was really an active volcano that had chosen to erupt on New Year's Eve, launching lava coated rocks for miles in every direction. Each explosion was deafening and echoed off of the valley walls, creating an exciting surround-sound effect.

When the final blast of fire had burned itself out and the last bomb had burst, the sound of cheering filled the air, like a college football crowd celebrating a home touchdown. The Elders clapped firmly, but evenly, while Samantha yelled, "Woooohoooo!" in excitement. Taylor managed to clap a few times, stunned by the power she had just witnessed.

"That was an amazing show," she murmured.

Gabriel laughed. "That was just the beginning."

While he was still laughing, four more tiny flares were launched. They exploded simultaneously, at the exact same altitude. Four distinct balls of tiny red twinkles of light formed haphazardly and then, as if by magic, moved together, transforming into some sort of a pattern. Within moments, the nature of the shape was clarified. A massive, four-headed dragon appeared—fully three-dimensional, the dragon was complete with four sets of sharp teeth and a barbed tail.

The beast hung in the air for a moment, before charging for the mountainside. The mythical creature was gargantuan—so large, that when it reached the cliffs, one of its four heads was able to peer into the cave where Taylor and her friends were watching from, while the rest of its body stretched to the ground, thousands of feet below. Taylor watched in awe as the mammoth seemed to make direct eye contact with her.

She was mesmerized by the deepness of its eyes—they seemed real, life-like—until the dragon reared back its four heads and with an explosive burst, shot fire from its mouths into the demon crowds. Most of the now-frightened onlookers shrank back from the flames, despite their natural immunity to fire; some even tried to flee back into the Lair. Within their little cave, everyone jumped back, including Gabriel, who tried to pull Taylor with him.

But she managed to wrench her hand free and remain seated, staring into the dragon's eye while the false flames washed over her. She felt a tiny tickling sensation over the entirety of her skin, like someone with a hundred hands was using a hundred feathers to tickle every part of her body simultaneously. She began to laugh and couldn't stop, even after the imitation fire had fizzled out and the dragon had faded away into nothingness.

While she laughed, her friends crept back to the edge of the cliff from the various safety positions they had assumed. Chris had grabbed Sam and thrown his body on top of hers, hoping to shield her from the flames. Gabriel and Sampson, not sharing the demons' protection from fire, and having grown up under the tutelage of angels that taught them to fear it, were the furthest back in the cave, ready to spring down the stairs if necessary. Kiren had slid to the side wall, flush against the rocky canvas. A few of the demon Elders had toppled over backwards in their seats, and even old Clifford had ducked, throwing himself flat on the ground, like a soldier under enemy fire. Only Taylor remained, sitting cross-legged on the blanket, laughing her head off, sounding madder than a certain Hatter in a particular Wonderland.

Gabriel rushed back, and asked, "Are you okay?" possibly mistaking her case of the giggles for some strangely delirious evidence of pain or shock.

She looked at him, trying to understand the question. Finally, her mind registered what he was asking. "Of course. That was amazing, don't you think?"

Gabriel was dumbfounded. "Amazing?" he asked.

From across the cave mouth, Clifford started chuckling. All eyes locked on the oldest demon on earth, who had seemed to catch Taylor's contagious case of the giggles. In between his deep, throaty laughter, Clifford managed to say, "Hoo hoo, of all the battle-tested, tough as nails, ice water in their veins, angels and demons in this room, hoo hoo hoo, it is the young human girl who is the bravest!" His laughter continued and soon the funny-virus was airborne and had afflicted all within reach of his voice.

Typically reserved demon Elders were rolling on the ground, their sides shaking; Samantha was laughing so hard she looked like she might pee herself; tears were streaming down Chris's and Sampson's cheeks; Gabriel was laughing heartily. Taylor joined in the fun, too, and carried on her laughing, free of fear for the first time since Gabriel and Sampson had brought them the news about the missing angel spies.

❦

When the next fireworks began blasting away the night sky, they, one by one, snapped out of their laughing fits, dried their eyes and cheeks, and, trying to catch their breaths, turned their attention back to the show. Gabriel was happy. He put his arm around Taylor and pulled her close. He whispered, "I love you, Taylor."

She turned and gazed into his nearly-black eyes, and replied, "I love you, too, *lommel*."

He looked at her, perplexed, trying to work through her words like they were a puzzle. Unable to make sense of it, he asked, "What's a *lommel*?"

Taylor laughed and spelled it out for him: "L-O-M-L—lommel."

Still not getting it, Gabriel just looked at her, unblinking.

Pausing after each word, Taylor explained, "Love… Of…My…Life. You're Iommel."

At this small revelation, Gabriel felt such an overwhelming degree of love and happiness that he found it hard to believe that less than a week ago he had been festering away in a dark, dank prison cell, with nothing to look forward to but a swift and painless death. *Oh how quickly things can change*, he marveled to himself. He pulled her closer and they turned their attention back to the entertainment. Everyone was happy, and seemingly safe for the moment.

What none of them knew was that a few important truths had been woven into the last few minutes of their lives: Taylor was even braver than Clifford had given her credit for, the fullness of their laughter represented the great calm before the storm, and things could, and most decidedly would, change quickly and without regard for those in the path of the huge and sometimes destructive wheel of life.

In fact, everything was about to change. And soon. Not tomorrow, or the next day, but right then.

Sixteen

After another twenty minutes or so of mind-numbing and ear-shocking explosions of aesthetically-pleasing eye candy, the atmosphere went dark. A light breeze purged the sky of any lingering traces of smoke. It was time for the grand finale.

A few minutes of silence followed, and then a booming voice resonated across the valley. "I hope you've enjoyed the 2010 Demon Spectacular!" Raucous cheers and whistles erupted from the mountain below. The voice continued: "Please enjoy the grand finale and remember to volunteer for next year's show, planning starts at the beginning of April."

Silence retook the night and all eyes transfixed on the sky, expecting greatness. A bright spotlight shone on the flat valley floor below. The beam of light fixed on a large cannon, sitting alone and unmanned. A sparkle of light flared near the main entrance to the Lair as a large fuse was lit. Burning quickly, the twisting, turning, fiery snake made its way to the lone cannon. As the igniter approached the ancient weapon, Taylor held her breath—she wasn't the only one.

The cannon ignited and, with a spurt of flame, fired *something* into the air, an object of some sort. The object was long and seemed to be sheathed in a thick, white mantle. Rising high in the sky the bundle reached its peak, and the covering fell away, revealing the true horror hidden inside. The audience stared in shock, as shimmering white wings spread forth from the now-glowing object. Realization set in as murmurs began to crop up through the crowd. Starting as whispers, they became louder and louder until someone yelled, "It's an angel!"

At that moment, the angel's legs swung backwards and it rocketed through the air. It was heading directly for "the best seat in the house," as Chris had earlier referred to their little cliff cave.

This time, Taylor allowed Gabriel to drag her to her feet. She felt herself being pulled against the wall. The group parted in the middle, like crazed fans at a rock concert allowing their idols to pass through them. Seconds later, the streaking angel crash-landed with a thud in the center of the cave. The angel nearly smashed its head off of the roof as it passed by them, and then skidded to a stop. Even Taylor, with her limited knowledge of angels and demons, knew that something wasn't right. The angel was dead.

Seventeen

Sampson rushed to the angel, who was lying face down on the ground and, checking for a pulse, confirmed, "It's dead." Turning it over, he gasped when he saw the face. "Oh, please, no," he croaked. His head dropped, his shoulders slumped, and he covered his head in his hands. "Noooooooo!" he screamed, the sound partially muffled by his palms.

Approaching the body, Gabriel looked over Sampson's shoulder. He quickly identified the face. "It's Boyd Chance. Dammit."

Wanting to know the significance of this particular angel's death, but trying to be respectful, Taylor said softly, "I'm so sorry, Gabriel. Who is Boyd Chance?"

When both living angels remained silent, Clifford surprised her by responding. "He was one of our spies. We recruited him about a year after Sampson."

Sampson finally looked up from his hands and stared at Clifford. A single tear dripped from his eye and painstakingly began the descent down his fractured cheek. His cheek was not physically fractured, but mentally and emotionally torn—his face was contorted in pain, agony. "No," he contradicted, "I recruited him. This is my fault."

Clifford said, "We all had a hand to play in this good angel's death. We must not let his efforts go to waste. There are another twenty-six angel spies trapped in that mountain." He pointed out of the cave mouth, towards the steep mountain to the west. "Given what's just happened, we can now assume that they have all been detected and will be executed swiftly. We must save them."

Gabriel turned to speak, but as he opened his mouth, the angels' mountain suddenly pulsed with bright, white light. Brighter than the powerful floodlights of an international airport at night, the valley was now fully illuminated; visibility was as good as it would be under a noonday sun on a cloudless day. Several demons screamed on the mountainside below. A voice echoed across the wide expanse, projected by a powerful microphone and speakers.

"You have now seen what we are willing to do," the voice boomed. Taylor recognized it immediately, but it was different somehow.

The voice of Dionysus continued: "We will do whatever it takes to reclaim what was ours. *Whatever...it takes*," he repeated. *Whatever.* The word had an ominous ring to it. Taylor realized what was different about his voice. From her experience with the Head of the Archangel Council, Taylor had found him to be shrewd, clever even. His voice was usually dripping with propaganda. She would describe him as snakelike. Since she had met the evil leader of the angels, Taylor could probably count on one finger the number of *true* things he had said to her. His words were generally heavy-laden with lies—he said whatever was needed to ensure he got what he wanted. Now, hearing his vague threats, she knew he was telling the complete and utter truth. Abandoning his propaganda, Dionysus was ready to hit the demons, along with Gabriel, Taylor, and whoever else stood in the way, with whatever would hurt them the most.

In this case, what would hurt the most would be the death of the traitors who had forsaken their own kind and pledged their loyalties to the enemy. In short, he would execute the angel spies.

"They're going to kill them!" another demon yelled from below.

Clifford, the demon Elders, and Taylor and her friends scrambled to the side of the cliff, leaving the young Boyd Chance lifeless on the cave floor. Sampson was the first to see the horror that lay beyond them: Dozens of angels were tied to stakes with fiercely bright ropes. From this distance, Taylor's mere human sight was unable to extract any details about the situation, but Gabriel, using his superhuman senses, locked in on the scene with the precision of high-powered binoculars. He recited what he saw like he was reading an intelligence report.

"We've got twenty-five...no, make that twenty-six angels tethered to two-foot diameter, titanium rods, using highly angel-proof lashes, wrapped around their arms and legs. There are at least two dozen guards, armed with blasters and light-swords. There is no sign of Dionysus; he is probably just speaking from the Command Center."

Coincidentally, upon mention of Dionysus, the echoing voice returned. "We know you have *the girl* in your custody. Return her to us immediately, and none of these angels have to die. We will allow them to cross over into your mountain, to fight with you, and to die with you as they see fit." The voice paused, and then said, "You have five minutes to choose."

Gabriel evidently didn't need five minutes. He said, "Sampson, Chris, Kiren—let's take care of this now. Obviously, we are not going to give them Taylor, so there's no decision to make. As Clifford said, we have to save them." Sampson nodded firmly, clearly agreeing with Gabriel's idea.

"No!" Taylor objected. "I will not watch my friends get slaughtered because of me. I will go willingly."

Gabriel responded quickly and strongly: "Taylor, I know you mean it and that your heart is in the right place, but let us do this. We are trained for situations like this and have a good chance of getting out alive with some of the angel prisoners."

"Some!?" she shouted. "I will not have my own life be the cause of *anyone's* death. Not angel, demon, or human. Not even gargoyle. I will go."

"Wait!" Chris and Kiren said simultaneously. They both looked at the wise, old leader of their race, who had remained silent thus far, preferring to listen to the discussion.

Chris asked, "Clifford, what should we do?"

Clifford sighed mightily. "It is a curse to live during such evil times, but I do not regret the burden I have been given, because it is also a blessing to have the opportunity to do so much good. Taylor, your courage is heartening and refreshing. I fear that most girls your age would sacrifice their own mother to spare themselves any semblance of pain, especially the risk of death, yet you willingly go, like a lamb to the slaughter. You are truly remarkable. I hope, and fear, that it will not be your last act of bravery before the War is won.

"However, you cannot give yourself to the angels, as that will all but ensure their victory—in their hands, the power within you is far too dangerous. You saw what happened the last time. We lost a lot of good men and women." He paused to collect his thoughts. The clock was ticking: Three minutes had elapsed since Dionysus had issued the time-based ultimatum.

Taylor took the opportunity to make another suggestion. "Then I must die," she said firmly. When Gabriel started to interject again, she silenced him with a hand and said, "Until I am either in the hands of the angels, or dead, your enemy will terrorize you. They will kill you and anyone that helps you. As you just pointed out, if I end up in their hands it will mean the end of life as we know it. Therefore, the only option is for me to go quietly into the night, to a better place. At least that is a contribution that I can make."

Clifford was already shaking his head. "No, that is also not an option. The angels will just find another person, with another powerful aura, to take your place. For now, we must try to use the fact that they are focused on you to our advantage. But that is a topic for another time." *Four minutes had passed, only one remained before the executions.* "Now we must act quickly and we don't have time to assemble a task force, so we must rely on the angels and demons in this cave. I will stay with Taylor and Samantha, as my duty requires, but must request the assistance of the rest of you for this important mission.

"I certainly would never force any of you, as it will be highly dangerous, but ask you now for your support."

Chris and Kiren immediately raised their fists in the air, using the demon sign of agreement. Gabriel and Sampson followed their example. To Taylor's surprise, the five demon Elders followed with fists of their own; they were willing to risk their lives—unlike the members of the Archangel Council who rarely considered going into battle—even though they would be outnumbered.

Clifford watched Taylor closely as if she might, at any time, throw herself off of the cliff and onto the jagged rocks below. Taylor knew she was being watched and was half-considering doing just that. "Taylor, the decision has been made. Do we have your support?" Clifford said. *Thirty seconds left.*

Taylor looked at her friends as they stared back at her. She looked at Samantha. Their eyes locked and more understanding passed between them than could have been communicated in a thousand words. Perfectly synchronized, the two human girls raised their fists in the air.

"Good, now go!" Clifford shouted.

Gabriel barely had a chance to kiss Taylor on the cheek before he leapt from the cliff, plummeting towards the earth. Sampson followed with a swan dive. Just when it seemed certain that her angel boyfriend was having a wing-malfunction, his magnificent, ivory, feathery limbs burst outwards and he soared high in the air, much faster than a bird. Chris pecked Sam on the lips and then was gone, having teleported beyond sight. Following his lead, Kiren and the Elders began vanishing, until only Taylor and her best friend, along with Clifford, stood watching the valley below.

Eighteen

Clifford raised a radio to his lips and ordered, "Get everyone inside and assemble the army!" He looked at Taylor, who was watching him curiously. "Just in case," he explained.

"Look!" Samantha exclaimed. Taylor saw that both flying angels now had passengers, most likely Chris and Kiren, who had teleported onto their backs, clutching at their feathers to keep from being thrown off by the force of their speedy flight, like cowboys riding bareback with only the horses' manes to hold on to.

Taylor felt powerless against what was to come. And she was. Whether she stood here and watched, ran back into the depths of the Lair, or even threw herself off of the mountain, it would all be too late to save them now. *Maybe they won't all die*, she thought. Her mind didn't permit her to be any more optimistic than that. Not at this moment.

In contrast, Sam said, "It will be alright, Tay." She squeezed her hand in support.

Seconds later, barely within the five minute limit mandated by Dionysus, the two angels and their passengers arrived at the first line of would-be executioners. The angels with the blasters and light-swords were ready for them. But they weren't ready for the demon Elders.

Appearing out of thin air, the five Elders already had their fire-swords extended and slashing towards their surprised enemies. One second elapsed—five dead angels. No more than twenty to go.

The remaining angel guards recovered quickly, firing pulses of light from their blasters, aiming at the pairs of flying angel-demon warriors. Gabriel banked sharply, narrowly avoiding the threat. Chris jumped from his back, landing on a female angel and thrusting his own sword deep into her chest. Gabriel grabbed another angel and slammed him to the ground, simultaneously stealing his blaster and pumping him with ten rounds of light. While the light rays wouldn't kill an angel, they would stun him long enough for them to carry out their mission.

Against all odds, they were winning. What they didn't know was that, for the angels, the fight hadn't yet begun.

Nineteen

Clifford had given each of the girls a pair of powerful, black binoculars that he had brought for viewing the fireworks. Now, they watched in suspense, as the battle continued. With each enemy that was struck down, they reacted as if they were back at college watching the UT Beavers decimate their opponents, cheering and high-fiving. Clifford, using a third pair of binoculars, watched tensely beside them, unspeaking. The radio was in his hand, and he seemed prepared to send in reinforcements at the first sign of a problem.

As Taylor was watching the scene unfold before her, out of the corner of her eye she noticed something glint, just a tiny sparkle as something metallic reflected the beams of the angels' bright spotlights. Then it was gone. She rotated her view to center on where she thought she saw the flash of light. There was a large, familiar-looking boulder, and then she saw it again, a brief twinkle of light; if she had blinked she would have missed it.

Using the zoom function on the binoculars to get an even closer look, she switched to 200-times magnification, aiming directly at the spot where she had seen the last flash. Sure enough, protruding from the large boulder was the metallic tip of something—a weapon most likely. "It's a trap," she whispered under her breath.

"What did you say, Tay?" Sam asked.

"It's a trap!" she yelled, much louder this time.

Clifford looked up, baffled by her sudden outburst.

"I can see someone hiding. Look to the right of the gate. There is a large boulder, someone is behind it."

Clifford and Sam tried to locate the exact spot she was referring to. They soon found it and saw the same glint that she had noticed.

Clifford said, "Maybe there is someone there, but that hiding spot couldn't possibly provide capacity for more than a handful of angels."

"Trust me on this, Cliff," she said firmly, using the casual form of his name, much like Sam. "There is a secret path there. It isn't huge, but the entire angel army could potentially march out of there, minus the gargoyles, which would need to use the main gate. Trust me," she repeated. "Sound the alarm."

Trusting her, he raised his radio to his lips and said one word: "Mobilize."

Twenty

Via their combined efforts, they had made quick work of at least half of their enemies, and the remaining angels were looking frightened and unsure of themselves, circling together in an effort to mount a well-formed defense against the vicious attackers.

Wanting to finish the job, Sampson charged the circle with reckless abandon. Ten blasters instantly fired on him and, while he was able to deflect four or five light rays with his sword, his body absorbed the rest of the firepower. He crumpled to the ground. Immediately, Gabriel, Chris, Kiren, and the five Elders jumped in front of Sampson, protecting him from further damage.

Although they were obviously winning the fight, Gabriel was acutely aware that they had not yet freed any of the captive angel spies. Because they didn't have time to formulate a strategy before the battle, they had all been fighting individually thus far. *It was time to work together*, Gabriel thought, as a simple plan formed in his mind.

"Demons," he said, loud enough for Chris, Kiren and the Elders to hear, but low enough that the angels wouldn't be able to make out his message, "distract the enemy and I will free the birds."

The demon warriors nodded in agreement and then charged into battle. Not like a human would charge, by running towards the enemy, or even like an angel might charge, by flying, rather, the demons began teleporting wildly at the angel guardsmen, popping in and out of view rapidly and in all directions. The angels fired haphazardly around them, hoping to get lucky and hit one of the demons just as they appeared. They were used to this particularly attack strategy, as the demons frequently used it in battle. Nevertheless, it had the desired effect: the angels were momentarily distracted.

Gabriel took the opportunity to soar into the air and then land softly next to the first of the angels in the line of captives. While the gleaming ropes prevented an unarmed angel from breaking free, Gabriel's light sword easily sliced through the knots that secured the angels' arms and legs.

As soon as the glowing tethers fell away from her frame, the angel collapsed, unable to hold her body weight with her wobbly legs. Gabriel reached out, and with one arm, caught her before she hit the ground. Her eyes fluttered open and gazed at him.

"Gabriel?" she said questioningly.

"Yes," he replied. He recognized her, but didn't know her name. "What happened to you?" he asked gently.

She opened her mouth slowly; her lips were chapped and cracking. Her eyes closed again. She needed water. "We were beaten and then bound." Her eyes snapped open, as if the horrors she had endured were being replayed in her mind. "They clipped our wings, Gabriel."

Dread filled him but he forced his voice to remain steady, confident. "Don't worry about that now. First we are going to get you all out of here. Stay here," he commanded, although he could tell that she wouldn't be able to get far on her own anyway. He was about to move onto the next prisoner, when a loud horn sounded from somewhere in front of him. It came from the mountain.

Twenty-One

Soon after Clifford gave the order for his troops to mobilize, Taylor heard the angels' horn sound. The trap had been unleashed.

Taylor had been watching Gabriel rescue the first of the prisoners, while keeping an eye on the secret path behind the boulder. When the horn sounded, angels frantically spilled out of the hiding space, some flying, other running at super-speed. They were all heavily armed.

At the same time, the main gate to the Lair was lifted and the demon army poured out, in no particular formation as was their trademark. There was no possibility that, on foot, the demons would be able to reach the front lines of the battle before the angel attackers. Thankfully, they had the ability to teleport.

Clifford raised the radio again, and started to say, "Teleport—" and then stopped abruptly. Something had caught the corner of his eye. With a loud war cry, hundreds of angels flew from the top of the demons' mountain, high above them. Many of them landed on top of the demon warriors, slashing with swords and blasting with guns. A melee ensued, as the chain of command was disrupted and it became every demon for his or herself.

Taylor watched in terror, as the demon army was forced to fight for their lives while, at the other end of the valley, the angel attackers were closing in on Gabriel and the other would-be rescuers.

Twenty-Two

When he heard the horn, Gabriel knew they were in trouble. He had only freed one captive thus far and, given the condition of the prisoners—clipped wings, unable to even stand on their own—they would need to fly, or teleport, all twenty-six of them to safety, along with Sampson, who was incapacitated and in need of medical attention.

Then he heard a roar from behind him and turned hopefully, expecting to see the full power of the demon army teleporting in to help them. Instead, he saw a sky full of angel hunters, zeroing in on their prey. *They were all alone*, he thought.

Not one to dwell on bad luck, Gabriel sprang into action, running at full angel speed along the line of prisoners, slicing twice as he passed each of them, freeing their arms and legs. Having no other choice, he let each of them slump to the ground, some of them wincing in pain from the impact. The added aches and pains from each fall would be minimal compared to what would happen to them if he didn't get them out of there soon.

When he had unfettered the final angel, he saw the first of the angel sneak-attackers honing in on him. He pretended not to see him coming, and then at the last second he ducked under the killing strike that was aimed for his head, and deftly slashed his own blade at the attempted murderer. The angel fell to the ground with a *thud*, but another had already taken his place, slashing violently at Gabriel.

Twenty-Three

Taylor watched the trap closing in on her friends. Samantha said, "We have to do something." Her usually calm and collected eyes blazed with fear. The situation seemed hopeless.

Clifford was pacing across the cave; he seemed unsure of what to do. Taylor had never seen him like this and it scared her. What could *they* do? *They were just human girls*, she thought. Then, like a lightning strike, Clifford's words from earlier pierced her mind: *The power within you is far too dangerous*. She was not just any human girl. She was *the one*. The one who was destined to end the War. It seemed that both the angels and demons had assumed that she could only help the angels to win—because only angels were able to harness her power—but no one had considered the possibility that a rebelling angel could instead use her against the angel army. Even she had not considered that possibility, but now it seemed so obvious that she nearly screamed it at the top of her lungs.

"Use me!" she shouted.

Clifford stopped his pacing to stare at her. Taylor's words didn't seem to register, so she said more firmly, but less loudly, "Use me, Clifford. The power within me, I mean. Use me."

Clifford appeared to understand what she meant and raised his eyebrows, surprised that he had not considered the notion. "But who?" he asked, searching her eyes for something he couldn't quite grab ahold of.

"Gabriel," Taylor said simply. "He's done it before, we practiced back at school. It's our only hope."

Clifford's head jerked up, as if his sudden understanding gave him a shock of electricity. "Okay, here's the plan. Sam, you stay here. Taylor, I will teleport you as close to Gabriel as possible, but then I will teleport out just as quickly. You have to get to him and convince him to use you as a weapon. I suspect this will be quite difficult, given you will be in the midst of a battle and he will be reluctant to put you in any danger, especially after what happened the last time. His first instinct will be to fly you out of danger, but you cannot let him do that, as it will mean sure death for everyone else. Is that understood?"

Taylor nodded, her brown eyes never leaving Clifford's—they were intense and penetrating.

"Okay, hold my hand."

Taylor reached out and clutched Clifford's hand, squeezing much harder than was necessary. She heard Sam say, "You can do this, Tay," just before she closed her eyes and evaporated into thin air. After feeling the *whoosh* and the twisting-turning feeling that she still hadn't gotten used to, Taylor opened her eyes and waited to return to real life.

Clifford's aim was near-perfect, and when she reemerged in the valley the first person Taylor saw was Gabriel, who had just cut an enemy angel to the ground with his sword. "Go, now!" Clifford ordered, pushing her firmly from behind. Before she had a chance to respond, he was gone.

Taylor ran in a half-crouch towards the love of her life, hoping to avoid instant death by an angel blaster—dozens of orbs of light filled the sky. In her peripheral vision, she could see Chris and Kiren using their own fiery swords to deflect the deadly light rays, while fighting the nearest angels. They were outnumbered and their enemies were beginning to surround them. Taylor's ability to get to Gabriel was their only hope.

When she got within ten yards, Taylor yelled, "Gabriel!" It was obvious that he heard her—his head perked up and there was a change in his fighting style, an urgency to swiftly defeat his current opponent. Gabriel pushed the angel back into a group of ten more attacking angels, momentarily throwing them off balance and allowing him to follow the sound of Taylor's voice.

He whirled around and, in less than a second, had scooped her up and leapt into the air, wings fully extended and undulating, as they raced across the sky. "No!" Taylor cried. "You have to *use me*! I am the only hope!"

"I'm not going to lose you again," Gabriel said firmly.

Taylor clutched his face with her hands, tilting his chin down, until his eyes met hers. She could almost feel the heat of the fire in her eyes. "Use me, Gabriel. You know you can. They will all die if you don't. Let me do this."

❧

Upon hearing her words, Gabriel's heart split in two. He had vowed he would never allow her to be hurt again, *used again*, but he also owed these angel spies, as well as the demons, his life. Taylor *was* his life, so putting her at risk was logically a fair payment if it was done for the greater good. And she had volunteered. She was doing it for him, for Samantha, for humanity. She was being brave...and he had to, too.

Abruptly, he stopped in midflight and accelerated back in the direction they had just come from. "Hold on!" he yelled, his voice rising above the sound of air rushing past them and the noisy fight below. Moments later, he landed next to a very surprised Christopher, who was fighting back to back with Kiren, who was standing overtop of Sampson, protectively. The demons were completely surrounded now, and on the verge of being taken hostage, at best, and being killed, at worst.

Ignoring the battle around them, Gabriel ordered, "You all need to teleport out of here immediately. Get the rest of the demons at the gate to do the same. Once we've cleared the field, teleport back out with some of your friends and grab the prisoners."

Chris looked at him like he was crazy, but, while blocking jabs from an enemy angel, said, "Consider it done."

After getting confirmation from Chris, Gabriel shot back into the air and out of the melee, trusting his demon friend to handle the rest. He soared for the empty center of the battlefield; thus far, the entire fight had taken place at either end of the valley. He knew they had to work fast and were relying heavily on Chris to get everyone out of harm's way. Dionysus would quickly realize what was happening and would either order a retreat, or send the full cavalry to kill Gabriel and Taylor.

Twenty-Four

Chris wondered how Gabriel planned to *clear the field*, as he had put it. He also wondered how in the hell Taylor had ended up on the battlefield and why Gabriel had not flown her to safety yet. However, with the world collapsing upon them, he had no choice but to trust Gabriel's judgment.

While Chris was thinking about his encounter with Gabriel, Kiren yelled to him. "I'll take care of Sampson, you worry about the Elders," she said, while holding off two angel attackers with her short, fiery daggers. She touched a foot to Sampson's unconscious body and vanished, along with him; she likely took him directly to the Lair's medical center.

Chris performed a dangerous, short-distance teleport to get closer to the five demon Elders, who were fighting at least a dozen angels. Teleporting at such close range was risky, because it gave less time for him to change his trajectory if he was going to miss his target landing spot. In a worst-case scenario, one could accidentally teleport into the same space being occupied by someone else, thus intermingling body parts with each other, like Siamese twins. Chris, however, had performed such maneuvers countless times in battle, and was able to appear within a few feet of the nearest Elder without incident.

He yelled, "We all need to teleport out now!"

The nearest Elder asked, "But what about the mission?"

"We've done our part, the rest is in Gabriel's hands," Chris said.

"Okay, let's do it. Move now!" the Elder commanded. Like a light bulb that unexpectedly burned out, all six demons disappeared, their enemies left swinging bright swords at the empty air.

Twenty-Five

Dionysus was enjoying this very much. Through the impenetrable, one-way Command Center glass viewing booth, he was able to use his super-human angel eyes and ears to watch and listen to the reactions of his enemies in their cliff cave. He saw and heard every moment: he witnessed the dead angel's crash landing, heard Sampson's miserable plea, and watched their horrified faces when he made his announcement about executing the filthy angel spies.

It was a rare opportunity indeed to see the head of the Demon Elders in such a precarious position, but of everything, he most enjoyed the verbal sparring of Taylor and Gabriel when she agreed to give herself back to the angels. He certainly never expected the demons to give Taylor back that easily, but for just a moment, he thought they might do just that. Instead, Clifford did exactly what he expected them to: He sent Gabriel and his friends to try to free the prisoners. Now they were about to be crushed in a perfectly laid trap.

Once Gabriel was his prisoner again, Dionysus was confident he could convince Taylor to turn herself in. If there was one thing that Dionysus had learned over the years, it was that love was a powerful force. And he was more than willing to exploit its power whenever possible.

He focused his attention back on the battle, and he watched Gabriel break away from the demons towards the angel prisoners. As instructed, the angel guardsmen allowed him to reach the captives unobstructed. *Now was the time.* "Initiate the trap," he commanded.

Commander Lewis, his second-in-command, radioed in the order and then they watched as the real fun began. Dionysus was impressed with Gabriel's hand-to-hand fighting ability and he allowed himself to reminisce about how different things might have been had Gabriel not been turned by the demons. *Ahh, the power of love*, he reminded himself. *Oh well, he could still find a use for Gabriel*, he thought.

The tide was slowly turning and he knew Gabriel would be captured soon. That's when something completely unexpected happened. Two new forms appeared on the battlefield, one disappearing again almost immediately. Even without his super-sight, Dionysus knew instantly who it was: *the girl*.

It was almost too good to be true, and because of this, Dionysus, usually quick to act, was mesmerized for a minute as he watched Taylor run to Gabriel. The Head of the Archangel Council snapped out of his trance when he saw Gabriel lift her off the ground and race back towards safety. *Damn*, he thought. *It was too late.*

Just as he was about to order some of his attackers to chase after Gabriel, he saw him turn around and fly straight for the heart of the battle. "What is he doing?" Dionysus hissed under his breath.

He was speaking to himself, but Lewis heard him and asked, "Who, sir?"

Dionysus looked at the Commander sharply, startled by his question. He locked stares with him. "The target of this entire mission, who do you think?" he reprimanded angrily.

"Oh," was all Lewis was able to mumble, clearly taken aback by the fierceness of the rebuke.

Lewis walked away, jabbering into his radio about capturing Gabriel before he could escape again. Dionysus watched him for a second and then, turning his attention back to the fracas, he saw Gabriel land next to the two young demons and say something to them. He couldn't make out what was said, probably because Gabriel was using his powers to block any eavesdroppers. The kid was smart, he had to give him that.

When Gabriel sprang back into the air with the girl, Dionysus could hear Lewis shouting orders into the radio, instructing all available personnel to chase him. There was nothing he could do but watch.

To his surprise, the demons teleported away from the fight just as Gabriel landed in the middle of the battlefield. *Something wasn't right.* Then it dawned on him: Gabriel was going to use the girl against him. With Commander Lewis still yelling various attack commands into the radio, Dionysus frantically charged towards him, tackling him to the ground. He wrenched the radio from his hands, pressed the talk button, and ordered, "All units retreat. Imminent threat detected. Retreat!"

Twenty-Six

Taylor craned her neck to try to see what was happening in the battle at the angel gates, but could only see flashes of light and swarming bodies. With his angel-vision, however, Gabriel was watching intently, waiting for the right moment.

He spoke quickly. "Okay, Chris and the rest of them are out. I'm going to try to shoot high enough to avoid the angel prisoners, but low enough to destroy the angel army. I'll try to be gentle, but brace yourself anyway," he instructed.

Taylor sat down and pulled her knees to her chest and then wrapped her arms around her legs. Satisfied that she was in a safe position, Gabriel lifted a couple of feet off of the ground, using his wings to hover in midair. He pointed an arm towards Taylor's balled-up body. Immediately, she felt the tingling sensation that she had experienced when he had first connected with her aura back at the University of Trinton. It was a completely different experience than when the angel snipers had nearly sucked the life out of her just a few weeks earlier. This time, in stark contrast to the agony she had experienced—it had felt like her soul was being ripped from her body and with it, each of her internal organs—this was a pleasant feeling. She couldn't help but laugh, as the feeling was like being tickled with a feather under her feet. Her body glowed softly, along with her nine rings, her ankle tattoo, and presumably the snake tattoo on her shoulder, until she looked more like an angel than a human. The glowing became brighter and brighter until she was forced to close her eyes.

Gabriel extended his other arm towards the now-confused angels that had tried to trap him and his friends while attempting their daring rescue. Just as he was about to fire the weapon, about half of the hundred or so angels burst upwards into the air upon receiving an order from the Command Center. Likely the order was to *Retreat!* or *Get the hell out of there!* as Dionysus realized what was happening. The other fifty angels were not as quick, or lucky.

From Gabriel's hand, a wide pillar of light swarmed across the battlefield and into the dozens of stunned, earth-bound angels, instantly vaporizing them. As planned, Gabriel managed to generate the base of the light-pillar a few feet above the ground, which he hoped would spare the lives of the weakened angel spies, who, in their current state, were unable to get to their feet. Gabriel watched cautiously as the angels who had managed to avoid instant death flew directly back to the mountain, in full retreat. His gaze lingered on the retreating angels for a few seconds longer to ensure they didn't try to double back, and then Gabriel rotated 180-degrees to take stock of the battle at the demon gates.

Where's the battle? was his initial reaction, but then, realizing that Chris had once again fulfilled his role by getting all of the demons to teleport out of harm's way, Gabriel fired the weapon once more, this time higher, into a flock of ascending angels. They had clearly also received the order to retreat and were caught in midflight while trying to escape. The angled light-beam cut down scores of enemies before fading away, leaving the night sky empty in its aftermath.

There were still hundreds of angels taking flight, but they had managed to spread out sufficiently to decrease the effectiveness of the weapon being used against them. Gabriel randomly charged and fired the weapon two or three more times, eliminating a few dozen more enemies, and then he followed the survivors with his eyes until they had been absorbed back into the mountain.

He waved his arm once in the direction of the Lair, signaling Chris to start the rescue operation. Rapidly, his concern switched back to Taylor, who had fallen over and was lying in the fetal position. Thinking she was injured, he rushed to her side and gently brushed her hair from her face. When she opened her eyes, he asked, "Are you hurt?"

The warmth of her smile filled his heart with relief. "That was incredible," she said. If he didn't know better, he would almost think that she was talking about another part of their relationship. Curious to talk to his girlfriend about what she was feeling, but wanting to get to safety as soon as possible, he gently lifted her body in his arms and soared into the air. As they rose, the bright floodlights were extinguished by some unknown angel technician, once more restoring the night to its natural state of darkness.

Gabriel looked back once and could still see twenty-six softly glowing forms, evidence that the angels spies were still there where he had left them. As he watched, however, the lights began to disappear in bunches, until there were none left. *Mission complete*, Gabriel thought.

Looking back at Taylor's still-smiling face, he said, "We did it."

She replied, "I couldn't be happier. We make a great team."

Under the light from the soft glow of his natural skin, Taylor looked even more stunning than usual. Her face radiated love and he knew that his own face reflected back the same love. Unable to hold in his curiosity any longer, he asked, "Why does it make you happy when I use your aura, but cause you so much pain when another angel does?"

They reached the cliff cave where they had started the evening; it was now deserted, as Clifford had likely teleported back into the Lair to monitor the aftermath of their unexpected mission. He had taken Samantha with him.

Gabriel lowered Taylor's feet to the ground and put his arms around her waist, searching her eyes for the answer. Her arms remained around his neck, clinging to him. "You don't know?" she replied. "Couldn't you feel it?"

Gabriel tried to remember what it felt like to connect with her aura. In the heat of the battle he was more focused on strategy: hitting his enemies, protecting the prisoners, etc. He hadn't been very in-tune with his feelings. But now, as he looked into the beautiful brown eyes of this intriguing and fearless girl, his feelings came rushing back to him: warmth, love, mercy, happiness, satisfaction. It was a smorgasbord of the best feelings that life had to offer and he, like Taylor, immediately knew the answer to his question.

"Because you are my soul mate," he replied, answering his own question.

She smiled. "Exactly, and you are mine. My *lommel*."

Gabriel sighed, kissing her deeply. When they pulled away, he said responsibly, "I guess we should get back inside to debrief the mission."

"I don't think they'll miss us just yet. I think we've earned a little alone time," Taylor said, pulling his shirt off. She tugged him to the cave floor.

He couldn't argue with that. "Lommel...," he said softly, wrapping his arms around her.

PART III

"To all my friends, present, past and beyond
Especially those who weren't with us too long
Life is the most precious thing you can lose
While you were here the fun was never ending
Laugh a minute was only beginning

Ever get the feeling you can't go on
Just remember whose side it is that you're on
You've got friends with you till the end
If you're ever in a tough situation
We'll be there with no hesitation
Brotherhood's our rule we cannot bend

When you're feeling too close to the bottom
You know who it is you can count on
Someone will pick you up again
We can conquer anything together
All of us are bonded forever
If I die you die that's the way it is"

Pennywise- "Bro Hymn"
From the album *Pennywise (1991)*

Twenty-Seven

Seething fury rippled under his seemingly calm exterior. A raging fire tore through his bones, burning into the very marrow of his being. How many lives did Gabriel have? He didn't care that a few of his angels had been killed—they were replaceable. What really pissed him off was that *his weapon* had been used against him. The demons had dangled the ultimate prize right in front of his face, like a matador waving a red flag at a snarling bull, and then whisked it away, leaving him as the foolish, snorting bull.

Stay calm, he thought.

Dionysus sat cross-legged on a mat, in a bright, empty room. He was meditating, trying to channel his anger and frustration in a positive direction. So far it wasn't working. The anger relentlessly boiled up, dangerously close to overflowing. He took a deep breath. Under his breath he repeated, "Anger is wasted energy," over and over again until his wrath had subsided. All he needed was a new plan. Something to focus his energy on. Something to rally his troops behind.

How do you draw a rabbit out of a hole? He, of course, knew the answer to this foolishly simple question: bait. But he had already tried using the angel prisoners as bait and, while the result was not as he had hoped, he still believed the strategy to be sound. He just needed more concentrated bait. But who? The answer popped into his head rapidly, probably a result of the intense level of focus that meditation gave to him. He smiled evilly, sprang to his feet, and rushed out of the room. A day and a half had passed since the New Year's Eve massacre and he knew that the Council was growing restless. It was time to call a meeting.

Twenty-Eight

Their New Year's celebrations had been ruined by Dionysus, but the successful rescue of the angel spies gave them a new reason to celebrate. The twenty-six ex-prisoners, each in various levels of deterioration, had recovered quickly, their superhuman angel bodies responding well to a day of rest, proper food, and lots of water. Their clipped wings had been replaced with the latest in titanium wing technology until their natural limbs were regrown. A feast was planned for the second evening from their rescue.

The loss of one of their own, Boyd Chance, was mourned at first, but then instilled in each of them a steely resolve to see their rebellion through to the end. Without being asked, each angel spy vowed to continue their fight against Dionysus, the Archangel Council, and all who supported them.

Gabriel and Taylor, along with the others who had participated in the dangerous mission, were debriefed by Clifford. The strategy going forward had yet to be determined, but endless accolades were poured out upon Taylor, to which she responded, "No biggie."

After the debriefing, Sampson was embarrassed. "I can't believe I was the first one down, how pathetic," he muttered.

"Yeah, pretty bad, man," Gabriel agreed.

Chris decided to join in on the verbal pile-on. "If it wasn't for Kiren, you'd be mince-meat. She stood over you like she was defending her first-born child."

"Kiren has a kid?" Sampson asked, looking concerned. It was impossible for him to hide his interest in the dark and tenacious beauty.

"Don't listen to them, Sampson," Kiren replied. "I am single, childless, and I thought you performed admirably as my steed. You protected me by taking the hit for me."

Sampson smiled sheepishly at the compliment.

Unfortunately for him, it just added fuel to the fire. "Geez, even after the battle is over, she is still stuck defending you," Gabriel taunted.

Trying to negotiate peace, Samantha said, "From where I was watching, you all would've been screwed if it wasn't for Taylor."

"True," Chris said. "Thanks again, Taylor."

Taylor frowned at Sam, irritated that she had turned the spotlight back on her. "Listen up. I don't want to hear anyone thank me, compliment me, or say anything else nice to me that is related to what happened on New Year's Eve."

"Looks like someone woke up on the wrong side of the bed," Sam said, giggling. "But, please. Indulge us just one more time." Taylor looked at her confusedly as her friend extended her arms like she was conducting an orchestra. "One, two, three," she said, and then, when she raised her arms, the ragtag gang of angels, demons, and humans said in unison, "THANK YOU, TAYLOR!"

This time Taylor didn't get mad. Instead, she couldn't help but shake her head and laugh at the five beautiful individuals standing before her. While they were all physically attractive, she felt that the beauty inside them far exceeded the quality of their outward appearance. A little cliché, maybe, but nevertheless true. The dynamic of the group was interesting. Not only because it was comprised of a mix of three different races, each linked by evolutionary forces, but also because of the length of the relationships.

Taylor and Sam had been best friends for years, but had only been with Gabriel and Christopher for a few months. Gabriel and Christopher, however, had known each other somewhat longer, having fought on opposite sides of the War. Likewise, Christopher had known Kiren, and Gabriel had known Sampson, since childhood, but Sampson and Kiren had only just met, and now seemed on a collision course with the first ever demon-angel romantic relationship. Lastly, Taylor and Samantha had only known Sampson and Kiren for a few weeks and yet they already felt as close to them as they did to each other's boyfriends.

Sam put an arm around Taylor, affectionately pulling her close. Taylor shook her off, pretending to look mad, but really she was glad to have her friend with her. Despite having Gabriel Knight, the love of her life, back with her, she knew that without Sam she would feel lost and alone. Sam always knew when to crack a joke, like just a moment ago. Taylor could only wish that she could ever provide as much support to Samantha as she received from her.

Still laughing at Taylor, Sam asked, "What should we do now?"

With a gleam in his dark eyes, Chris suggested, "Why don't we go say hello to the gargoyles? You girls haven't seen them close up yet, have you?"

Simultaneously, Gabriel and Sampson said, "No!" while Samantha exclaimed, "Yeah!"

"Why not?" Sam asked, when she heard that the angels' reply was opposite to her own.

Taylor replied, "We kind of forgot to tell you about our last close encounter with gargoyles." Taylor went on to tell about Sampson's brilliant idea to visit the angel gargoyle paddocks and how the gargoyle had nearly killed them all by connecting with Taylor's aura. While Sampson was partly to blame for them being there in the first place, he recovered some of his pride when he told, in great detail, the part about how he and David, Gabriel's younger brother, subdued the raging beast before it could seriously hurt anyone.

"So you can see our hesitancy in going anywhere near a gargoyle again anytime soon," Gabriel explained.

Chris said, "I hear you, man, but that situation only turned bad because it was an *angel* gargoyle that was able to connect with Taylor's aura. Demon gargoyles, like demons, don't even have the ability to see the human aura, much less connect with it. I don't see any harm in taking them down there."

Gabriel looked like he was ready to punch his demon friend, but held his anger back when Taylor said, "Cool it. He's right, Gabriel. We won't be in any danger. It's completely different." After a few minutes of Chris describing the security measures in the gargoyle cages, the types of stone walls used, and the strength levels of the steel bars, he reluctantly agreed to give it a try.

Chris, always the leader while in the Lair, walked at the front, his arm linked with Sam's. He led them down a narrow, spiraling tunnel. Other than the demons, none of them had ever been in this area of the Lair before.

Taylor and Gabriel followed closely behind them; Gabriel kept putting his arm around her protectively and she kept shrugging it off. He could be so damn protective sometimes. She needed to find balance in her life. While she forgave Gabriel for his sins, she didn't want to go back to being just his girlfriend. She wanted to be herself: strong, resilient, tough, independent.

Following a healthy distance behind were Sampson and Kiren. Their flirting had picked up in the last few days and now, as their hands brushed against each other's casually while they walked, they chatted more privately, their voices hushed as they spoke in fierce whispers.

As they descended, the lighting became darker and darker until the frequency and strength of the torches declined enough to thrust them into darkness for long stretches of time. Already on edge, Gabriel's glowing lips moved up and down. He said, "Hey, demon-boy, is this really the way?"

Kiren laughed somewhere in the darkness behind them. She said, "Yeah, Chris. Isn't there a faster, less scary way?"

Chris admitted, "I thought the long way would be more exciting and suspenseful. We could have taken a transporter directly there, but that's so boring."

"Next time give us the option," Gabriel grunted. "We'll take the transporter back."

"Grouch," Taylor said, shrugging off another attempt by her boyfriend to hold her hand. She wasn't in the mood.

Chris snapped his finger and a healthy fire ignited in his palm, lighting the way. Sam said, "It never has to be dark with my not-so-human torch."

Taylor added, "Yeah, for me either, with my not-so-human glow worm."

The girls laughed together loudly, Chris sniggered, and even the right corner of edgy Gabriel's lips turned up in amusement. Not ready for the joke to die yet, Kiren rekindled the laughter when she said, "We've got both back here! Dionysus would die from the sight."

After another three—or maybe three hundred—turns in the tunnel, Chris stopped abruptly. Taylor inspected the tunnel around them. It was the same monotonous gray rough rock arching above them. "Why the hell are we stopping?" Taylor asked bluntly.

"We're here," Chris explained.

"Oh," Taylor replied, not understanding at all.

With a flourish, Chris waved his fiery hand towards the seamless, rock wall and then pressed his knuckles to the cold, textured stone. The grinding of gears and the clatter of chains resonated from somewhere within the mountain. Like something out of an *Indiana Jones* movie, a hidden door rose upwards, disappearing into the roof, revealing a well-lit chamber beyond. Taylor looked inside, expecting to see lifelike coats of armor and human skeletons walking around, as if possessed by ghosts. Crossing the threshold, she cringed, anticipating the sting of poison darts and preparing to run if a massive boulder crumbled from above, ready to flatten all those who dared to trespass.

When none of her imagination's darkest creations proved to be true, she relaxed, although she found that she had instinctively gripped Gabriel's hand. She quickly released it, horrified at how easily she fell into the boyfriend-girlfriend trap that she used to always make fun of.

"Let me introduce you to some of my favorite gargoyles," Chris suggested, sounding like a zoo tour guide ready to introduce a family of gorillas to an excited group of kids. "I think, Taylor and Gabriel, you've met the first one. On your left is Freddy."

Taylor squinted, and was barely able to discern a large, black shape through the gloom.

Noticing her inability to see in the dark, Chris said, "Sorry, I always forget that humans don't have the same capacity for night vision as we do." He touched his torch-hand to a notch at the side of the thick, metal bars, and Taylor watched in awe as the flame travelled across the whole of one of the cell walls, fully illuminating the space.

In one corner stood a hulk of an animal. It stared at them suspiciously, clearly startled by their presence and by the unexpected flair of fire in his cave.

"Freddy…," Taylor murmured.

Seeing the angels, Freddy became agitated, stomping his feet, gnashing his teeth, and flapping his humorously inadequate wings.

Sam asked the obvious question: "What happened to his wings?"

Chris smirked and looked at Gabriel. "Care to answer, *angel-boy*?"

"Let's just say we didn't see eye to eye on something," Gabriel responded furtively.

An answer like that was never enough for Sam, and after a couple minutes of nagging, he eventually told everyone the entire story from what felt like an eternity ago: Taylor being hunted by Freddy, Gabriel's daring rescue, and the necessary destruction of Freddy's wings to incapacitate him.

"Why was it necessary to rip out his wings?" Sam asked.

Chris answered for Gabriel. "Short of killing it, the only way to quickly stop a gargoyle is to remove its wings. That sounds like an easy task, but I can tell you from experience, it isn't. Even with our superhuman strength, most angels and demons would struggle to quickly incapacitate a gargoyle."

Sam nodded. "Okay, but how does Mr. Freddy have wings now then."

"They grow back eventually, it takes about a year. Because the attack on Taylor was a couple of months ago, the wings have a long way to go, which is why they look pathetically small. But even when they are full grown, gargoyle wings appear to be far too small to allow them to fly, but trust me, they are sufficient."

"Yeah," Taylor agreed. "I thought I had outrun the damn thing and then like some winged freak, it swooped down behind me, with drool hanging off of its fangs, stomping around like it was Godzilla."

"Hey! Not everything with wings is a freak," Gabriel objected.

"Oh, sorry, birdman," she joked, "I didn't mean you."

Sam was more interested in the details of the story. "That's intense, Tay. How close did you get to him?" She motioned to Freddy the gargoyle.

"Let's just say he was close enough that I could smell the filthy reek of his bad breath; it smelled like he had been eating onions and garlic all day and not brushed his teeth. I was more worried about dying from nasty odor intake than I was from being mauled."

Sam sniffed the air expectantly. "I see what you mean, this entire place smells like bad B.O."

"Nah, that's just Sampson, did you forget to put on your Nivea deodorant again, man?" Gabriel joked.

Sampson was not about to back down on this one. "Wait a minute. How is it that you are trying to make fun of me, Gabriel? I thought we agreed that as compensation for me being such a straight-arrow, stalwart of goodness, defender of humans, and you being such a devious, lying, puppet for Dionysus, you weren't going to give me a hard time anymore?"

"Ouch, man, straight through the heart." Gabriel feigned like he had been shot with an arrow. With a performance equal to that of Cruise or Pitt, he struggled to pluck the "arrow" from his chest, eventually succeeding in wrenching it from his flesh. Clutching his breast, he sank to his knees and then keeled over, dead as a doornail. The entire group was in stitches by the time he regained his feet and gave a small bow. "Anyway, Sampson, I only agreed not to tell old stories about you, but I don't remember anything about not joking with you. I feel like that is part of our dynamic, what makes us friends."

"True, buddy," Sampson laughed. "I was just hoping to be able to take shots at you for a while without getting anything in return."

"No hope for that," Gabriel replied.

Sampson shrugged. "Oh well, what's next on this comedy gargoyle tour?"

They moved onto the next cage. As they walked, Chris explained how the cages were staggered—one on the left, then one on the right and so on—so that the gargoyles didn't have a direct line of sight to each other. Gargoyles, by nature, were afraid of being alone and so, by keeping them separated, they were easier to work with, less likely to act up.

"Do the parents have any interest in them?" Sam asked.

"Not really," Chris answered. "They are bred more for their fighting ability—they are absolute killing machines—than for their companionship. There are only a handful of demon couples. Most demons go for humans, with whom they can have demon children. But in the rare instances where two demons fall in love, they are asked whether they would be willing to breed gargoyles for battle. Most of them accept it as a responsibility, but once the baby gargoyles are born, they leave them in the care of the army."

"Seems a bit cold," Taylor suggested.

"I see where you are coming from, but unfortunately, it is a necessary evil. The angels breed gargoyles like rabbits, and so we have to do the same to ensure we don't get overpowered in battle."

"It's true," Gabriel confirmed. "The angels' gargoyle breeding program is completely out of control. Every day they get more and more angel volunteers to participate in the program." He didn't try to justify it.

"If this war is ever over, I would do everything I could to change things. No creature should be bred to die," Taylor said.

"War makes all beings do stupid and disgusting things," Chris conceded. Clearly trying to change the subject, he said, "And on your right is a brand spanking new gargoyle family. As you can see, not all gargoyles are bred from two demons, many of them are bred from other gargoyles. In this case the mom, Belinda, and the dad, Prince, have created young Rocky here."

Taylor peered through the bars while Christopher once again lit a wall of fire for the humans. Between the large stumps of legs of the full grown male and female gargoyles, Taylor watched as a tiny, dinosaur-like creature peeked out at them, its black eyes barely visible in the fire-lit cell. Like his parents, Rocky had short, stubby arms and thick legs. His body was inky-black and covered in scales. His open mouth had tiny sets of razor-sharp teeth that already looked capable of shearing an arm, or even a leg, from anyone that got too close. But what truly captivated Taylor were his eyes. They were so fully black that they appeared to be a void of darkness, sucking the light from the immediate area around them. And yet, they sparkled. The contradiction was so poignant that Taylor found herself unable to shift her gaze from them. When he saw the group staring at him, he quickly withdrew again, seeking protection behind his father's right leg.

"Aww, he's a cutie!" Sam exclaimed.

Prince let out an agitated snarl, and a short burst of fire plumed from his strangely-human mouth. Belinda followed suit, stomping her feet and snarling furiously.

"I think it's time to move on," Chris suggested. "Their parental instincts are kicking in. We usually try to stay away from newborns for at least a month. They develop remarkably fast and once they do, the parents will lose interest in them entirely, allowing them to make their own way in the world."

※

They continued along to the next cell. "This one is Mr. Magoo," Chris said. "Despite his not-so-tough-sounding name, he is our oldest gargoyle and by far, the toughest in the lot."

"How old is he?" Gabriel asked.

"Two years old," Chris said proudly.

"Impressive. Ours, I mean, *the angels'* gargoyles have never made it past a year," Gabriel explained.

"Really? Their life spans are that short?" Sam asked.

Chris grimaced. "Well, not exactly. While not as long-lived as any of us, gargoyles can last a good forty to fifty years if they stay out of trouble. Having a forty-year-old gargoyle was very common in the early-1900s, before the angels evolved. Now their main purpose is for war, and most of them are killed off quickly and replaced." Chris expounded all of this with a pained expression on his face. And after Taylor's reaction to some of the other information, he said it pensively, expecting another negative reaction. Instead, there was only silence.

Chris looked around. "Where's Taylor?" he asked.

Gabriel swiveled his head side to side while saying, "What do you mean? She's right beside me…At least she was…"

"She's still looking at the baby gargoyle," Kiren said, looking behind them.

Sure enough, Taylor was crouched, low to the ground, her hand reaching through the bars of the Prince-Belinda-Rocky cell. Quickly realizing the situation, Chris yelled, "Taylor! Don't move. Pull your hand away slowly and then get to your feet and move away quietly."

Anticipating Gabriel's move to save his girlfriend, Chris put his hand out and stopped him. "Any sudden movement may provoke the parents. Wait for her to get clear." Not looking convinced, but trusting his friend who clearly had more experience with gargoyles than he did, Gabriel remained still, but was poised to spring into action if necessary.

Taylor said, "Don't worry, it's okay, guys. They like me." She had turned her head to look at them when she said this, but now turned back to the cage. She spoke in a gentle, high voice, like you would speak to a baby, or a dog. "Aren't you the cutest little thing? I want to take you home with me. Protect you from these mean angels and demons," she cooed.

They watched in surprise as a tiny head poked through the bars and Taylor stroked it softly. Her mannerisms appeared as normal as if she were petting a dog; only she was rubbing an animal that could only be described as grotesque when it was full grown, albeit rather cute at this early stage in its life.

"Stay here, guys," Chris instructed, making eye contact with Gabriel to ensure he would obey the instruction. Gabriel looked worried, but his eyes showed that he would let Christopher handle the situation.

Chris walked slowly over to Taylor, who was now sitting cross-legged on the ground. Every few steps he paused to survey the scene ahead and ensure that the parents were emotionally stable. To his surprise, when he got close enough to see completely into the fiery chamber, the parents seemed completely at ease, more so than when they were merely being observed. Now, Taylor was actually handling their young child, and they seemed to be fine with it.

Taylor turned, and seeing Chris, said, "What do they eat, do you think he'll eat out of my hand?"

Bewildered, Chris replied, "I'm not sure that's a good idea."

"It will be fine, trust me," Taylor said.

Sure, trust the human girl who had only had two previous experiences with gargoyles, both of which resulted in the gargoyles trying to assault her and having to have their wings forcibly removed, Chris thought. But then again, these ones did seem to like her. Chris tiptoed over to an arched opening that was hewn into the rock wall. He tried to be as quiet as possible because, while he was feeling more and more comfortable that Taylor was not in any danger, he was still worried that his presence might anger Prince or Belinda or both.

From a small storage room he retrieved a few strips of cured, preserved meat. As he handed the meat to Taylor, his eyes vigilantly jumped between Momma Gargoyle and Papa Gargoyle, watching for any signs of a change in their moods. "They're carnivorous," he said. "They go through a lot of meat and typically we only feed them at regular meal times, but I guess we can make this one exception."

"Cool, it's like beef jerky," Taylor commented, accepting the strips of meat.

"It's actually very similar," Chris agreed. "We give them large steaks for dinner, but these are more of a treat for good behavior."

※

Taylor held out a ribbon of meat and Rocky eagerly snapped it up. His pointy fangs made short work of the beef and he swallowed with a gulp, seeming almost human in the process. He enthusiastically pushed his chin further through the bars. Taylor did not disappoint, flipping shreds of meat into Rocky's open mouth. Even if her aim was a bit off the mark, Rocky would, with lightning quickness, adjust his head to the side or downwards to catch every single one. The game continued until all of the meat had been devoured by the scaly eating machine.

"You are such a good little eater," Taylor clucked. She rubbed him behind his very human-looking ears. "Can I keep him?" she joked.

Chris laughed. "No, but he does seem to like you. I would be happy to bring you down here to see him from time to time, although I must warn you, he will grow up fast and he may lose interest in you soon."

"Sounds great, thanks, Chris," Taylor said, standing up and following him back to the others. Rocky's parents had barely moved during the entire exchange.

When they approached their friends, Gabriel strode forward and hugged her tightly, "You had me scared there for a minute, Tay."

Pushing him away, she looked up at him with amusement. "Oh, don't be so dramatic, it was fine."

"You didn't realize you were dating the gargoyle-whisperer, did you, Gabriel?" Chris joked.

Gabriel chuckled, but still looked weary, stressed, like the whole incident had aged him. Wrinkles formed on his brow and at the corners of his eyes. "Once again, I am duly impressed," he said.

"Don't be," Taylor said, "I just felt a connection with the little guy and acted on it. No big deal."

Gabriel said, "Let's get outta here. The celebrations upstairs will be starting soon and I would really like to see a few of my old friends now that they've recovered."

They all agreed that they had had enough of gargoyles for the day. Taylor winked at Rocky as they passed by his family's cage on the way out and she swore he winked back at her. "Did you see—?" she started to ask Sam.

"See what?" Sam asked.

Not wanting to sound crazy-obsessed with the baby gargoyle, Taylor thought better of her question. "Never mind, it was nothing."

Sam looked at her like she was crazy anyway, and then put an arm around her, walking several strides while hugging her. "You're a funny one, Taylor Kingston, but I'm glad we're here together."

"Whatever," Taylor said, trying to maintain her unemotional facade. Sam rolled her eyes.

Gabriel reclaimed his walking partner from Sam and she went back to Chris's expectant hand. Taylor watched as a truly happy expression formed on Sam's face when her fingers intertwined with her boyfriend's. Under the firelight, Taylor's hand found Gabriel's too, on her terms this time, and she looked into his deep, black eyes, which were rimmed by a mere sliver of blue. She marveled that she and her best friend had found such true and unconditional love at nearly the exact same time in their lives.

What would the future bring? She dreamed of a normal, happy life. Well, almost normal. A few midnight flights on Gabriel's back, using Chris's ability to teleport to tropical dream vacations—they would have the best of all worlds: human, angel, and demon, in perfect harmony. And that future could be theirs! It could be theirs if they could just survive the present.

Twenty-Nine

Andrew paced across his brightly-lit room. Ever since he and the other Archangels had left Mount Olympus, a sense of foreboding had filled his every waking moment. Mount Olympus was the name given to the compound that Dionysus had constructed to protect the Archangel Council from the demons. As long as the Council and Dionysus as its Head were there, sufficiently removed from the front lines, Andrew had felt he was able to control the situation. Since they had moved to the mountain, just a stone's throw from the battlefield, Dionysus had acted with reckless abandon—attacking in broad daylight within sight of humans, conducting a spy witch hunt, and executing prisoners. After the latest Council meeting, Andrew was convinced he had completely lost his mind.

It probably all started when Gabriel Knight—the golden son, he who delivered *the one*, the future of the angel cause—had betrayed Dionysus and helped the girl to escape. On that day Dionysus's eyes were wild with anger, like Andrew had never seen before. The evil lurking behind those eyes must surely have been born from the Devil himself. That's when Andrew's fear began to rise.

For years he had known that the Head of the Archangel Council was evil, and thus, Andrew's conscience led him to a secret meeting with Clifford Dempsey, the head of the demon Elders, where he pledged himself to the demon cause—the protection of humans. Over the last decade, Andrew had passed on information to the demons that was so valuable that he may have singlehandedly prevented Dionysus from taking control of the world on numerous occasions.

The most important piece of intel was The Plan, Dionysus's ultimate goal, which was known only to the Council and to a handful of other key angels, and thanks to Andrew, of course, known to the demon Elders. Knowing that with the demons out of the way, Dionysus would kill off most of the human race and enslave the rest to use as a source of eternal life for the angels, had helped provide the demons with a significant amount of motivation to win the Great War.

When Dionysus began the angel spy witch hunt, Andrew became fearful that he, too, would be discovered. He was not fearful for his own life, for he would gladly give it for such a noble cause, rather, he was fearful for the lives of his family: his wife, Sera, a human, and their three angel children, aged seven, four, and two. Dionysus had surprisingly shown mercy, if you could call it that, to the families of the angel spies who were discovered, by not convicting them to the same fate as their loved ones. However, Andrew knew that Dionysus would not be so merciful if he discovered the level of his treachery. His life, and the lives of his family, would be forfeit. An example would surely be made of him: Traitors Will Be Punished!

Andrew had been too scared to try to pass a message on to the demons about the planned New Year's Eve executions and related trap. But after seeing what evil had almost transpired on that night, how close the angels had been to winning their prize, he promised himself that he would find a way to protect his family while still fighting for what he believed in.

The first step was honesty with his family. He told his wife everything, and although their children were still quite young, the eldest being seven, she agreed that they could not risk their children's recruitment into the army. Preparations were made quickly, and Andrew's family, under the guise of a vacation, was moved to a safe location, far away from their home on Mount Olympus. In the coming weeks, new identities would be created for them and they would be moved again. All of these preparations were necessarily done over the phone, as Andrew would arouse suspicions if he took a trip away from the mountain during these pivotal days. While he knew that all phones within the mountain were monitored by Dionysus's personal security squad, he had a "clean" phone that he was able to use to avoid detection.

Getting his family to safety greatly reduced his fears, and now his attention was focused on the situation at hand. He continued to pace back and forth, thinking of how to proceed. If his room had had a carpet or a rug, rather than the shimmering white tiles, he surely would have worn an anxious path in the fibers. He did his best thinking while pacing.

Three hours earlier, the Council meeting had ended and Andrew had rushed to the bathroom, to vomit up the delectable lunch that was served prior to the meeting. The corn on the cob, Greek salad, and garlic shrimp, each made a disturbing reappearance; thankfully, he was able to reach the porcelain halo before the fireworks began. Going forward, he vowed to chew every bite into a liquid mush before swallowing, regardless of how delicious the food was, or how hungry he was.

Ever since his stomach calmed down though, he had been pacing...and thinking. No matter the risk, he needed to contact the demons before Dionysus executed his newest strategy. He couldn't allow the girl's father to be used for bait—it would destroy her.

Thirty

The after-New-Year's celebration went off without a hitch, and although everyone knew that somewhere deep within the angels' mountain some kind of a nasty plan was being concocted, for this night they were going to celebrate what they had to be thankful for: namely, their lives, and in particular, the lives of the twenty-six angels who had been recovered.

The feast took place in the rarely used Grand Dining Hall, which had been speedily decorated for the occasion. For their guests of honor, the recovered angel spies, a special table was set up at the front of the room. While light was still provided in classic demon style—by torch lamps and candles rather than by fluorescent bulbs like the angels—to commemorate the event, brilliant white wings and glowing statues had been placed throughout the Hall.

To kick off the evening, Clifford gave a wonderfully inspiring speech, during which he more than once embarrassed Taylor, but also showed great gratitude for the sacrifices made by everyone in attendance, from the angel spies all the way down to the demon weapon technicians. He demonstrated to everyone what a true and pure leader he was; there were no threats or spats of anger like his angel counterpart, only a genuine belief in their cause and the people carrying it out. Applause and cheers followed nearly every line of his unprepared speech, as every ear appreciated the goodness in Clifford's words.

He ended with a surprising prophecy. As he spoke, it was like he was in a strange trance—eyes staring straight ahead, rather than his typical, engaging style. His normally active hands hung limply at his side. The boisterous audience fell completely silent for the first time all night, captivated by the words that followed.

"The Great War that has plagued us for fifty years will not last another year," he declared. Clifford's voice was booming, echoing throughout the Hall; he had no need for a microphone or a bullhorn. "It is not clear who will be victorious, only that the end is near." His words had an ominous ring to them and more than one face flinched upon hearing them.

As quickly as his stone face had appeared, it retracted, leaving the animated and friendly face of the demon Elder. He looked down for a moment and then looked up sharply, his eyes clear and focused. "I don't know why I said that, only that it is true. I don't know if we will win the War, but I know that it can only be accomplished by the combined effort of those in this very room. It cannot happen by demons alone, but must be carried forth by demons, angels, and even humans." He winked at Taylor and Sam when he said the last part. "Raise your glasses," he commanded. Thousands of goblets went into the air. "May this be the year that the Great War is won, that humankind is protected, and that we begin a period of peace amongst all who roam this great earth!" Cheers erupted throughout the crowd, glasses clinked, and drinks were drunk. At least for this moment in time, Taylor felt a hope that had previously eluded her. It would be short-lived.

Thirty-One

After a night of food, drink, and fun, the six friends were walking back to their rooms with their arms around each other. Gabriel had had a few too many drinks and was talking more than he had in the last six months combined.

"I've done a losht of bad thingsh in my time, and sho have the rest of the angelsh, but the demonsh have done shtupid shtuff, too." His words slurred together and Taylor grimaced. She had never seen him like this. It was not attractive.

"Shut up, Gabriel. No one wants to hear it," Taylor said, tired of listening to his crap.

Ignoring her, he continued. "Like, who shent that Jonash guy to UT, anyway? He almosht got Taylor killed with that damn gargoyle." Taylor cringed at the reference to Jonas. He was definitely a mistake that the demons had made. Sending him and his posse to the University of Trinton was the main reason that Gabriel had felt backed into a corner, forcing him to give her up to the Archangel Council. But that was in the past now.

"He was just there to check up on Chris. The demon Elders were worried that I wasn't sufficiently protected from the angel Council." Taylor hoped this reminder would quiet her drunken boyfriend.

"That's not exactly true," Kiren interjected.

"What do you mean?" Taylor asked.

"Well, you know how I told you that I was there to keep an eye on things from right next door to you, as Marla's roommate?"

"Yeah," Taylor said, a bad feeling washing over her.

"Just before Jonas arrived, I sent a report to the Elders. I only stated facts, like how Gabriel was still dating you and spending more and more time with you, how it seemed like Chris and Gabriel had become friends, that kind of stuff. I guess the Elders interpreted it to mean they should send someone in, and they chose Jonas."

Gabriel stopped in mid-stagger. He glared at Kiren. "I'll kill you," he said, perfectly coherent now. Despite his drunkenness, he moved with lightning speed, his powerful fist crashing into Kiren's jaw. She flew backwards, like she had been hit by a freight train.

As soon as she realized what was happening, Taylor chased after him. Gabriel was poised to attack again when she reached him. Grabbing his clenched arm from behind, she said, "Stop it, Gabriel. Please, no more."

Coiled tighter than a spring, Gabriel's reflexes were faster than the sound of her voice reaching his ears. His elbow flung backwards, defending himself against what his muddled mind believed was an attack from behind. Taylor gasped as his powerful elbow connected with her chest and her body was thrown backwards.

Neither Chris nor Sampson had been idle during the sudden change in mood. Before Kiren's body ever reached the ground, the latter had caught her as gracefully as a wide receiver catching a touchdown pass. In one motion, he cradled her, placed her on the ground, and then stood over her, taking on a boxing stance, ready to defend her in the event of a subsequent attack.

Chris, on the other hand, put an arm across Sam's body, to protect her if the fight spilled towards them. However, upon witnessing Taylor's limp body being propelled towards the rough, rock wall, he teleported out in front of her, estimating the path of her flight. When he reappeared, Taylor smashed into his stomach, and despite his readiness, he toppled over from the impact. He grunted as she landed on him, her fall cushioned by his strong torso.

Lifting her head slightly, Taylor saw a very different Gabriel standing in the tunnel. All rage having melted from his face, he looked mortified. His shoulders slumped in defeat and he sank to his knees, mental anguish taking all of the fight out of him. "What have I done?" he moaned, rhetorically. "Taylor, I'm so…I'm so…"

Chris said, "There will be plenty of time for apologies, Gabriel. For now, go and get some rest and Sam and I will take care of Taylor. Leave now, man. Just walk away."

Gabriel tried to utter a protest, but Sampson grabbed his arm firmly and pulled him to his feet. "Let's go, man." Without further struggle, Gabriel allowed himself to be half-assisted, half-dragged by Sampson back to his room. For some reason Kiren followed after them.

Upon reaching his room, Gabriel sat on the bed, staring at the wall. Kiren thought he looked numb. Sampson started to leave, but Kiren lingered. "What are you doing?" he asked her. She raised a hand to silence him and went over to Gabriel, kneeling in front of him, submissive.

"Gabriel, I'm really sorry about Jonas. I really didn't mean for all that to happen."

Gabriel's eyes were moist as he dipped his head to look at her. "No," he said simply. "It wasn't your fault. I was the one…I was the one who put Taylor in this position; I was the one who couldn't stop it." He looked on the verge of a break down.

"Yeah, you made some mistakes, some really BIG mistakes, Gabriel. But you made up for them, and you are still making up for them now. Things could have been much worse if they had sent someone else to get Taylor, someone other than you. You saved her, in a way. But now you need to focus on your future with her or it will disappear. You have to forgive yourself. You have to forgive us for anything we might have not done perfectly. Anything less, and I promise you, she will leave you. Maybe not today, but some day." Kiren knew these truths would be hard for Gabriel to take, but he needed to hear them. There was still time for him to turn things around, and although he sometimes wore his heart on his sleeve, something told her that Gabriel Knight still had an important role to play.

Gabriel looked a bit shocked upon hearing the monologue by the demon he had just savagely attacked, largely unprovoked. His eyes were apologetic, soft. "I'm sorry for hitting you, Kiren. I'm really sorry," he said. It sounded sincere.

"That's a good start, buddy, and I forgive you, but tomorrow you will need to pander for Taylor's forgiveness, and she may not be such an easy sell. Then you can move on and do what needs to be done in this war."

"I will," Gabriel said. "Thanks for understanding me, Kiren."

※

Sampson had watched the entire exchange with wonder. He was typically not the type of guy to fall head over heels for a girl, like Gabriel or Chris had done, but his feelings for Kiren had been welling up inside of him since he met her, and hearing her now, he knew she was someone special. *Hopefully, his someone special,* he thought. He strode over and, standing behind her, put his arms around her neck. "Yeah, yeah, you're welcome, man, but we'll still have to vote on whether to invite you to our wedding," he joked. "I can't believe you hit my girlfriend!"

The tension on Gabriel's face eased slightly. "I didn't know it was official. Man, I didn't even have a chance to warn her about you."

Kiren looked back at Sampson. "I didn't know it was official either," she said.

"It is if you want it to be," he replied.

"I'll think about it."

※

When the two new love birds left Gabriel to sleep, he managed to get undressed and under the covers without feeling sorry for himself. He was completely sober now—

the emotions of the last hour were more effective than coffee in that regard. While mumbling, "Stupid, stupid, stupid," he smacked himself in the head with his palm. "Okay, think," he whispered.

First he needed to apologize to Taylor—that much was clear. But he also needed to give her a reason to forgive him. Wife beaters apologized for the black eyes, gambling addicts apologized for losing college tuitions, cheaters apologized for cheating. But those were empty apologies. He needed to be better than that, worthy of forgiveness. Before drifting off to sleep, the first steps of a plan began to form in his mind.

Thirty-Two

"How are you feeling, Tay?" Sam asked. She stroked her hair, like a mother tending to a sick child.

"I'm fine, I just feel a little bruised," she replied, gingerly rubbing her chest.

"I should say so," Chris said. "You took a hit from a pretty tough angel."

"Thanks for the reminder that my boyfriend hit me."

"It really was an accident, Taylor," Sam said. "I saw the whole thing."

"I know it was and I know that Gabriel would never intentionally do anything to hurt me, but the fact of the matter is, he was out of control and reckless. I really don't need that right now, considering my entire life seems out of control and reckless."

Taylor was lying on Sam's bed, while her friends sat on one side of her. Concern continued to lace Sam's expression. For a few minutes after Taylor had sustained the elbow to her chest, she was wheezing sharply, barely able to pull any air into her lungs. Initially, Chris had started to carry her to the medical wing, but changed his mind when Taylor's breathing finally returned to near-normal. "I'm fine, no doctor," she had gasped.

Taylor was worried that if she went to a doctor, hard questions would be asked and Gabriel would get in trouble. Also, given Gabriel's history, the Elders might kick him out of the Lair for good if they caught wind of his attack on Kiren and his accidental elbowing of Taylor.

"I understand," Sam said. "Do you want me to keep him away tomorrow?"

"No, I'll talk to him. It's not like I don't love him anymore. I just hate him sometimes, too."

"Ok, sweetie," Sam replied. "Now, get some sleep, it's been a long day."

"And you have something to look forward to tomorrow—you get to see Rocky," Chris reminded her.

At the mention of her scaly little friend's name, her mood brightened. "I forgot about him. Before breakfast I'd like to go down so I can feed him, if that's okay?"

"Of course. I'll stop by at seven o'clock."

Before the door had closed, signaling Chris's exit from the room, and before Sam had curled up beside her, Taylor was already asleep, dreaming of her new pet gargoyle and all the fun they would have together.

Thirty-Three

His "safe" phone to his ear, Andrew waited anxiously for his friend to answer. After three rings he heard, "Yes?"

At three in the morning, it was not surprising that Clifford sounded groggy, having likely been awakened mid-REM cycle. It was difficult for Andrew to wait until now to call him, but he knew it was safer. *For him. For his family.*

"I have unfortunate news, my friend." There was urgency in his tone that he could not disguise. "They will take her father. Good luck." With the message delivered, Andrew ended the call. They had done this enough that

Clifford would understand. Tonight would be a sleepless night for them both.

Thirty-Four

At first he had been angry at having been awakened at such an early hour. But after he was informed that Dionysus had requested his presence in his private chambers, he had been more than happy to go with the lowly guardsmen. Since his encounter with Gabriel during his escape, he had been itching to hear the six words that so casually rolled off of Dionysus's lips: "I have a mission for you."

When he heard what the mission was and how secret it was—being kept even from the other Archangels—he was ecstatic. Dionysus trusted him, and rightly so. He had a destiny to fulfill, which would almost surely entail playing a major role in ending the Great War. And it would all start with this one mission, a mission that would give him both professional and personal satisfaction.

Back in his apartment now, he was still licking his lips just thinking about the opportunity he had been given. Thankfully, he wouldn't have to wait long—the mission was to be carried out that very night. He had a lot of planning to do: selecting his team, coordinating the timeline, procuring supplies, contingency plans, etc.

His thoughts reverted to Gabriel—the traitor to his people, the human-lover, the demon-lover, the imbecile. Slamming his fist into the wall, he roared, "I WILL get my revenge!" The glassy, fluorescent wall smashed inwards, showering glass and sparks onto a table and two chairs. The light flickered and then went dark. Wrenching his hand from the wall, he gazed at the blood dripping off his knuckles. He watched as the flow of white blood slowed and then ceased entirely, the wound repairing itself in a matter of minutes.

He picked up the phone, pressed a button, and then demanded, "Send someone up to repair my wall immediately." He returned the phone to its cradle. *Being chosen by Dionysus really did have its perks*, Lucas thought.

Thirty-Five

As promised, Chris, along with Sam, knocked on Taylor's door at seven in the morning to take her to visit the gargoyle dungeons. This time they utilized the speedy transporter to get there, cutting the travel time in half, which would allow Taylor to spend more time with her new friend. During the ride, Chris continued to warn her that gargoyles were strange creatures and that they were subject to sudden mood swings and personality changes.

"How's that any different than us? Remember last night?" Taylor asked, rubbing her sore chest as a reminder.

Sam and Chris looked at each other and laughed. Clearly, they had been avoiding the subject, but Taylor was more than ready to face it head on. "What are you going to do, Tay?" Sam asked.

"Nothing. I'll just listen to what he has to say and then talk it through with him. That's what couples do, right?" Not that she knew. She had barely dated anyone in her life. But it sounded logical.

"I don't know, I normally just break up with my boyfriends if they act like jerks," Sam said.

"I guess I better watch my step," Chris replied. "I didn't realize it was one strike and you're out."

"Well, I guess for you I can make an exception. I'll give you two, maybe even three strikes."

"Wow, thanks, babe. I feel honored," he said.

"I think Gabriel will need quite a few more than three strikes if this is going to last," Taylor said.

Upon exiting the transporter, Chris led them straight through the security doors. First room on the right, Taylor remembered. She preferred to think of it as a room, rather than a cell, despite the bars over the door.

They passed Freddy, from whom loud snores could be heard in the otherwise quiet dungeons. Before they even reached Rocky's family, they heard a snort and then a scurrying of feet across the stony floor. A small head popped out between the bars and looked towards them. While it was hard to label expressions on the face of a gargoyle, Rocky actually looked like he was excited.

"Wow, Tay, he looks happy to see you," Sam remarked.

Chris said, "I've never seen anything like it before. Gargoyles are typically quite shy and never really get attached to anyone, not even their parents. He must have remembered your smell from yesterday and then come to greet you when he picked up the scent."

"I do not have a smell, or a scent," Taylor said.

"I didn't say a bad smell," Chris laughed. "Just a smell, in general."

Ignoring her demon escort, Taylor knelt down and said, "Hey, Rocky. Did you miss me, buddy? I definitely missed you. There's a certain angel upstairs that I'd like you to take care of for me, can you do that for me, Rocky?" She laughed when he tickled her hand with his long, wet, forked tongue, which snapped in and out of his mouth quickly, like a snake.

"Hmm, maybe it *would* be useful to have a pet gargoyle," Sam said. "You know, to help keep boyfriends from misbehaving."

"I heard that," Chris said, returning from the storeroom where he had gone to obtain some food.

"I'm just sayin'," Sam said.

Chris handed a tray to Taylor. It had various meaty-looking treats on it. Unlike the previous day, the meat was raw. He also gave her a padded glove. "What's this for?" she asked.

"A fire-retardant glove. Just in case," he explained.

"Oh, little Rocky won't hurt his Aunt Taylor, will you, buddy?" Despite what she believed, Taylor donned the glove before holding the tray out for the mini-gargoyle to munch on. She nearly dropped the tray when a ball of fire burst from his mouth and licked the food, causing it to sizzle and pop on the metal surface. The long glove was instantly warm from the heat.

"What the hell was that?" Taylor yelped.

Chris looked at Rocky curiously. "I don't know, but I think…"

"What?" Sam asked, looking at her boyfriend quizzically.

The tiny meat-fires died slowly and then Rocky opened his jaws wide and began scarfing down the food, barely even chewing. "I think he prefers the meat to be cooked," Chris guessed.

"Makes sense to me," Sam agreed. "I hate bloody meat. I'll take well-done every time. Except for sushi, of course."

"Is that strange?" Taylor asked.

Chris scratched his head. "Actually, very strange. I have never seen a gargoyle do that. Typically, they'll just gobble up whatever you put in front of them, like a garbage disposal. It seems Rocky here has very refined tastes."

"That's not surprising. Rocky is a very special gargoyle," Taylor remarked.

"It sure seems that way," Chris replied.

"Hey, where are the parents?" Sam asked. "Belinda and Prince."

Taylor looked up quickly; she had forgotten that Rocky even had parents. The back of the room was empty. Rocky looked even smaller in the bare room.

"Oh, yeah, I forgot to tell you guys. Apparently, after we left yesterday, the parents wanted nothing to do with their baby. They were making all kinds of noise, refusing to look at him, or go anywhere near him. So they moved them out. At this age, most gargoyles are very dependent on their mothers to care for them, but not Rocky. It seems he was too independent for them and they didn't like feeling useless, so they left him. When they left, he reacted positively, running around his cell and putting on quite a show for the gargoyle-tenders."

"You *are* special, little one," Taylor cooed. He had finished the food and now looked up at Taylor, who was stroking his head with a gloved hand. He appeared to be smiling, his mouth wide open, displaying rows of sharp teeth. But he didn't look threatening. Instead, his mouth looked comical—just a toothy grin from a playful pet. Taylor's hand drifted down his neck and onto his back.

"What are these?" she asked, her fingers lingering on two raised bumps on Rocky's upper back.

"That is the very, very beginning of his wings. Despite the fact that he is only three-days-old, he is already starting to mature, which is completely normal for them. We track the growth patterns of all of the gargoyles, from birth to death." Chris pulled a chart from a clipboard attached to the wall. Taylor hadn't noticed it previously, as her attention was fully focused on Rocky. Reading from the chart, Chris said, "As of this morning, he's three feet tall and was born at only two feet, so he's grown a foot in three days. In a week, he will be as tall as me, and in a month, he will be about as tall as his parents were and his wings will be ready for him to use."

"Wow," Taylor said, genuinely in awe of the facts she had just learned. "I guess you won't be my *little* Rocky much longer." Rocky made a sighing sound, as if he understood what she had said and wished it didn't have to be that way. "But I hope you'll always be my friend." He smiled at her and swished his little tail from side to side, like he was using it as a broom to clean the floor.

"We better get going, Taylor, we can come back later if you want to," Chris said.

Taylor scrambled to her feet and said goodbye to the always-happy Rocky, promising to visit him again soon.

When they stepped off the transporter, they all agreed that a nice, leisurely breakfast would hit the spot and then Taylor could have her "talk" with Gabriel. However, when they walked into the café, Gabriel jumped up from his seat, where he was sitting with Sampson and Kiren, and rushed to Taylor's side, in a panic. "Where have you been?" he growled.

Taylor frowned, the blood rushing to her face. "Listen, I don't think you have any right to be asking the questions right now. Not after what you did."

Gabriel cut her off. "No, you don't understand, there's some kind of an emergency. I think it affects you."

Taylor's face wrinkled in confusion. She said, "What the hell are you talking about?"

"There's an unscheduled Elders meeting in ten minutes." He looked at his watch. "Make that five minutes. They've been looking for you guys. We've been summoned and they said that most importantly, you needed to be there. I've heard a rumor that it has to do with your father, Tay."

Taylor's confusion turned to shock. "What does my father have to do with anything?"

"I don't know, but we will soon find out."

While Chris loaded up a bagful of almond croissants and berry muffins for them to eat on the way, Taylor's mind raced. How could her father be involved in anything that had to do with angels and demons? He was just a regular, boring old human.

Unconsciously, she followed Chris and her friends to the transporter, ignoring the constant looks from Gabriel. They arrived five minutes later.

When they walked in, they were already a minute late. The various discussions that were buzzing throughout the Elders' chamber ended abruptly and a hushed silence fell across the room. As usual, six chairs had been prepared for the guests of honor.

Before their butts had hit the chairs, Clifford pushed the meeting forward. "I have some troubling news for you, young lady," he said, directing his words towards Taylor. "Your father has become a target of the angels."

From what Gabriel had told her, Taylor already feared that her dad was in some sort of danger, so no surprise showed on her face. Instead, she wanted facts. "How do we know this?" she demanded.

"We have an inside source that is very reliable."

"I thought they had weeded out all the spies."

"Yes, all but this one. This one is near the top. That's all I can say."

Taylor's heart sank. When she became involved in the whole angel-demon war mess, it was a risk she was willing to take on her own. Because it was exciting; because she loved Gabriel; because it felt right. But she was never willing to risk her dad's life for it. "What are they going to do to my father?"

Clifford was not one to sugarcoat things. "Abduct him. Hold him hostage. Use him to get to you."

"When?"

"Tonight. As soon as we found out, we teleported a squad of twelve, highly-trained demons to protect him until we could conduct this meeting. In advance of tonight, we would like to add some additional protection for him."

Gabriel said, "I will go."

Before Clifford could respond, Taylor said, "No, you need to stay here with me. For support."

"I need to do this for you, Taylor."

"No, you need to stay here for me, Gabriel."

Gabriel looked at Clifford for backup—but he didn't get it. "Sorry, Gabriel, but in this case, I cannot go against her wishes. You will remain here. We will send Sampson, Christopher, Kiren and a few others, if they are willing."

"Let's rock," Sampson said. The two demons just nodded dutifully.

Gabriel looked frustrated, but managed to hold his tongue.

"If there is nothing else to discuss, this meeting is adjourned," Clifford concluded.

Thirty-Six

As she had promised, Taylor had called her dad each day she was away. Typically she tried to get off the phone as quickly as possible, mostly because she hated having to lie to him. She planned the daily calls in advance to ensure she was able to tell him lies that made sense; she was supposed to be vacationing in Florida, after all. The beaches that she said they went to had to be real, and she needed to research them so she had details that would make her stories more credible.

Today though, she couldn't bring herself to tell him another lie. She also couldn't tell him the truth; so instead, she focused on asking him questions about what he had been up to. Edward Kingston seemed excited that his daughter was suddenly taking such a keen interest in his life, and he took it in stride, describing in detail the weekend fishing trip that he had taken with James over New Year's.

"I'm surprised he went with you, didn't he have any plans for New Year's Eve?" Taylor asked.

"Yeah, I think so, but he cancelled them when I suggested the trip." Eddie spoke with pride in his voice. He was happy his son still had time for him.

"I'm sorry I didn't stay home for the holidays, Dad."

"It's really no big deal, honey. You accomplished a lot this year and I'm very proud of you. I wanted you to have this trip."

Taylor felt sick to her stomach. Here she was, completely lying to her dad, putting his life in danger, and he was being so sweet to her. She tried to speak, but her mouth felt dry, her lips parched. The words caught in her throat. There was so much she wanted to say to him, to thank him for. Her worst fears crumbled through her mind, like collapsing buildings. What if this is the last time she ever spoke to him? What if she never saw him again? What if James is there and they take him, too?

"Taylor? Are you there?"

Snapping out of her temporary depression, Taylor managed to croak, "I really love you, Dad."

"I know, Taylor. I love you, too. I'll see you in a week."

She hoped he was right. "Sure, Dad. See you soon. Bye."

Ending the call, she lay on her bed in the fetal position for what seemed like hours, but turned out to only be ten minutes. When she finally sat up, there was a determination in her eyes that had been absent since the meeting that morning. A steely resolve set in as she recited to herself, "Everything will be fine. Good will triumph over evil. Chris and Sampson will protect him."

Her mind wandered to Gabriel. Should she let him go with them? He would surely be an asset to the mission, and having him there may decrease the chances of her father being captured. But the selfish part of her wanted him to stay with her, to hold her and tell her that everything would be alright. Her mental debate was in full-swing when there was a knock on her door.

It was Gabriel.

"Can I come in?"

Wordlessly, Taylor opened the door wider and let him follow her over to a couch. When they had both sat down, Taylor said, "Look, I'm sorry I told Clifford you couldn't go on the mission."

Shaking his head, Gabriel replied, "I've been thinking…"

"That's dangerous," Taylor interjected.

Gabriel cracked a smile, and took the opportunity to put his hand on Taylor's leg, stroking it gently. Thankfully, her joke had sliced through the tension like a knife through butter. She even allowed him to touch her. Taking a deep breath, he continued, "I love you, Taylor, and I am willing to be whatever you need me to be. I would love to stay here with you, if that's what you want."

"I'm not sure it is, Gabriel. Dammit, I'm just so confused. I want you here with me, but if that means less protection for my dad, then I'm just being selfish. I don't want to be selfish."

His arm moved to her shoulder and then casually curled behind her neck, pulling her head into his chest. He kissed the top of her head, which made her wince, but she didn't pull away. "You have already proven you are not selfish, Taylor. You've risked your life to save the lives of others. Angels and demons who you don't even know. But you are only human…"

Now it was Taylor's turn to crack a smile. "Is it that obvious?" she joked.

"Sometimes it isn't, but you need support, too. You can't always be brave—you shouldn't always be. I am asking your permission to sit this one out and stay with you. I need a break in the action, too. And I trust Chris, Sampson, and the rest to protect your father. In fact, I know they will. In my mind, the absolute worst-case scenario is that they are forced to teleport him to the Lair to save him. In which case, we will just have to tell him the truth. I know I've learned that the truth is never a bad thing."

Taylor thought about it for a minute. The idea of telling her dad everything started to sound better and better. Gabriel was right—there was no way that Chris would allow the angels to kidnap her dad if he had the chance to teleport him away. "I guess that makes sense. Okay, I agree. You can stay."

"Now on to other matters, or have you forgotten?"

Taylor leaned her head back against Gabriel's chest to look into his eyes. Her face crinkled in confusion.

"Maybe I shouldn't have brought it up, your memory is terrible, Tay. How does your chest feel?"

"My chest? What is that, some kind of an awful pick up line? It's fine," she said, subconsciously massaging her chest with her hand. "Oww, crap, it's really sore." Then she remembered. In all the emotional trauma of learning that there was a threat to her father, she had completely forgotten about what had happened the previous night. "Oh, yeah," she snorted.

"I guess that means I'm not off the hook?" Gabriel asked.

"You abused your girlfriend. I might have to press charges."

"I'll claim temporary insanity," he joked back. "But seriously, I'm really, really—"

Taylor cut him off. "Stop, Gabriel. Do you know that you acted like an idiot?"

"Yes, but—"

"Good, and do you know that what you did was reckless and childish?"

"Yes, but, Tay—"

"Good, and do you promise not to do anything so stupid again?"

"Of course, Tay—"

"Then you're forgiven, end of story," Taylor finished, raising a finger to Gabriel's lips to shush him. She quickly replaced her finger with her lips, kissing him tenderly.

When she pulled away, Gabriel was still not ready to let the whole thing go. "I do *not* accept your forgiveness," he declared. Taylor looked at him like he was crazy. "Last night, I thought long and hard about what I did and decided that an apology and 'I won't do it again' is not sufficient to obtain forgiveness. I will not accept your clemency until I have played my role in defeating Dionysus."

Taylor smirked. "Whatever you say, angel-boy."

Thirty-Seven

Dionysus admired himself in the mirror. Attractive, powerful, clever: he had it all. Clever, oh so clever. His latest plan was pure genius. It would throw the demons into a panic, scare the hell out of the girl, and create a diversion, which would allow Lucas to easily accomplish his mission—the real mission. And the cherry on the top: He would be able to determine whether there was still a spy in their midst.

He had been too careless, too trusting. But he had learned from his mistakes and would not make them again. After discovering the extent of the treachery, Dionysus had spent hours poring over old mission logs and battle reports. Searching, searching—and eventually finding. After two days of extensive research, he had discovered at least twelve potential occurrences of leaked information. Leaked plans, leaked strategies, leaked decisions. And this treachery was not at the lower ranks; it was at the highest levels, within the group of generals, or even the Archangel Council itself.

He had trusted his chosen angels implicitly. Trusted in their belief in him, trusted in their support of The Plan, and most importantly, trusted in their hatred of the demons. But he had been wrong in trusting so freely.

And so, by devising a plan that would be known only to him and his new apprentice, Lucas, he could narrow down the search. Only the Council knew the full details of the feigned abduction of the girl's father. The generals and Commander Lewis were kept in the dark. If the demons were already there, protecting her father, then Dionysus would know that he had a mole in his most trusted group of advisors. He suspected as much. And he had a guess or two as to who it might be. Johanna never seemed to be on the same page as him. Or Sarah for that matter. There was something about her that he just didn't like.

He never should have allowed women on the Council. The men were solid, though. Michael was practically his brother, and he and Andrew went back many years—it couldn't be one of them. He would find out soon enough. And then there would be hell to pay.

Thirty-Eight

Unfortunately, the hours had passed by swiftly and it was time for the slow, torturous waiting to begin. Chris, Kiren, and a dozen others, including Sampson, had armed themselves and were about to march to the teleportal.

"Be careful, babe," Sam said, giving her boyfriend a big hug.

"I will, don't worry," he replied.

"Give 'em hell," Gabriel said to Sampson.

"You know me."

"That's what worries me," Gabriel joked.

The two angels embraced and Taylor could see that this was a very difficult moment for Gabriel. He wanted to be with his friend, doing something to help. But she dared not suggest that he go, for fear that he might actually listen to her for once.

It was time for them to go.

Taylor, Gabriel, and Sam stood with their arms around each other, as they watched their friends depart down the tunnel.

"You should start practicing," Gabriel said cryptically.

"For what?" Taylor asked.

"For the speech you are going to have to give your dad when they bring him back here. That is going to be one tough conversation."

Sam said, "Your dad likes me. Just let me do the talking."

"You always do," Taylor joked.

It helped to laugh. The next few hours were going to be difficult, but it would help if Sam and Gabriel were at their funniest.

"Let's shoot some pool," Sam suggested.

Thirty-Nine

Chris counted them down: "Five, four, three, two, one, go!"

The second defense unit teleported harmoniously to the drop spot. Kiren had held Sampson's hand, bringing him along with her. There were four other angels included as well—from the rescued group of spies. They had fully recovered and eagerly volunteered for the mission, ready to get their wings—or at least the prosthetic titanium wings—dirty again.

The landing spot was the Kingston's attic. Taylor had informed them that it was used only for storage and that no one ever went up there. Using the highest point in the house, they could set up the mission from a good vantage point on the inside. The attic was particularly effective because it provided a 360-degree view of the area around the house. It had windows on all four sides that were built into the slanted rooftop.

The first goal was to identify the twelve demons that were part of the lead squad and ensure they were positioned appropriately. Chris made swift work of the task using a thermal detector and his radio. "Blue squad leader, do you read me?"

"Yessir," a female voice replied.

"I am picking up sixteen thermal images in the vicinity, not including *the Cheese*, who appears to be the only one in the house. Can you account for the additional four heat sources?" *The Cheese* was code talk for Mr. Kingston, the one they were protecting.

"Yessir. The two small blips to the east are a couple of squirrels that live in the large oak tree. The third spot, in the backyard, is a stainless steel grill that the Cheese used to cook a couple of steaks thirty minutes ago—it is still warm. The final hit you are getting is a backup generator for the house, which kicked on ten minutes ago when the power went out. It seems that the Cheese is well prepared for emergencies."

"Why is the power out?" Chris looked out the window. It was a clear night, it couldn't be weather related.

"We don't know, but we are guessing it was the work of the angels as part of their strategy. I don't think they anticipated the house having backup power though. The Cheese has been on the phone with the power company twice now and they have confirmed that the power grid is fully functional and that it must be specific to his house. They said they would send someone out in the morning and he agreed. His generator will provide up to twenty-four hours of power and he can turn it off before he goes to sleep. He doesn't seem too worried."

"Good. Thank you, blue leader. Stay in position and wait for my orders."

"Roger that."

Next, Chris re-briefed his team on their positions. Their approach was highly aggressive and they had been authorized to use any methods available to protect Mr. Kingston, including teleporting him back to the Lair if necessary.

They would essentially litter themselves in and around the house, in various spots, getting as near to Taylor's dad as possible. If he got close to seeing any of them, they would simply teleport back to the attic. Sampson and the other angels, however, would position themselves on the roof, as lookouts, to make the best use of their wings if the attack came from the sky, which was considered very likely.

"Okay, move out," Chris said.

The demons teleported out of sight, leaving only Sampson and the other angels in the loft. Sampson opened a window and peeked into the backyard, two stories below. It was empty. "Clear," he said gruffly.

One by one, the angels crawled out of the window and along the shingled roof. Each perched so that they faced in a different direction to ensure the entire sky was covered by their watch. Ten painfully slow minutes passed. Then another ten. Halfway through the third ten, Sampson spotted something. "I've got a bogey approaching from the north. Might just be a bird, wait for my confirmation." He whispered sharply into his headset.

As the "bogey" approached, there was no doubt in Sampson's mind: it was an angel. A scout, most likely. "We've got a solo-flyer coming in slow from the north. Should I take him out?"

Chris replied, "No. Lookouts—make yourself scarce. We want them to think the house is unprotected."

Obediently, the rooftop angels hustled back through the windows, taking refuge in the attic. Sampson watched cautiously through the glass panes. The angel circled the house three times and then raced back in the direction from which it came. "Scout's gone," Sampson informed them. "Prepare for a full attack, I don't think they know we're here."

"Roger that. Stay in the attic and let us know what you see."

Sampson waited patiently. He didn't have to wait long. In less than five minutes he saw them coming. Lots of them. Not panicking, he counted them quickly and then announced evenly, "We've got eighteen targets coming in from the north."

Chris took charge. "Okay. We are going to surprise them. If all goes according to plan, they won't even step foot anywhere near the house. The lead demon squad and the angels up top will perform a synchronized attack, while they are still in the air. If any of them manage to get through you, we will handle them from the ground." Chris's orders were clipped, efficient, like he was merely reading through a grocery list. "Sampson, you've got the best view. You give the signal."

"Yessir."

His stomach squirming with anticipation, Sampson watched the angels soar, in perfect formation, towards the house. When they got within a hundred yards, he commanded, "Angels—go! Demons—follow in five seconds." Sampson wisely staggered the attack, allowing five seconds of flight time for his angels before the demons teleported into the fray. He hoped that the attack would be perfectly coordinated.

The angels burst out of the house and raced towards the incoming attackers. Seeing five angels roaring towards him, a look of surprise flashed across the lead angel's face, and he halted his team in midair. A second later, Sampson crashed into him shoulder first, generating enough force to knock a 747 off its flight pattern. At the same time, twelve demons appeared out of thin air, each landing on the back of an angel.

Having the element of surprise in their favor, the Sampson-led team quickly gained the advantage, knocking several of the angels out of the sky. The remaining angels turned tail and ran, or flew rather, retreating from the surprise attack. The five demon-friendly angels chased them for a few miles to ensure they wouldn't try to make a second attack. Finally, satisfied that the enemy was gone, they returned to the attic, where all of the demons were now gathered.

"Something ain't right," Sampson said. "That was way too easy."

Forty

While listening to the radio transmission from his team, Dionysus cracked his knuckles in anticipation. He had gathered the full Archangel Council together to monitor the situation. They sat around a long, glowing table in the Master's Room; the mission was being broadcast in full surround sound. They would be able to hear every word in clear Dolby Digital.

Dionysus looked around the room, sizing up his friends, or maybe his potential enemies. This was the moment of truth. If one of them was a traitor, then surely the demons would be protecting the girl's father. Each Council member seemed to be focused on the broadcast;

there were no fearful faces in this crowd. Dionysus frowned in concentration as the mission leader announced that they were within 500 feet of the target.

"400 feet, 300 feet. Wait, there's something emerging from the roof. Crap, there are five angels approaching us from the house. I can't make out their faces. Stop the attack!" the voice commanded, presumably to his team. And then: "Oomph, dammit…Who are—?"

"What's happening?" Dionysus yelled to no one in particular.

Various voices came through the speakers. They heard, "It's a trap!" followed by two screams and "I'm hit!" Finally, someone yelled, "Retreat! For God's sake, retreat!" The rush of wind whistled in the night.

Dionysus picked up a wireless microphone and raised it to his lips. "Is anyone there? Can anyone tell me what's happening?"

Ten seconds passed in silence. And then a frantic voice, bathed in static said, "We have nine down… ssshhh…knew we were coming…ssshhh…never had a chance."

"Don't bother coming back," Dionysus sneered into the microphone. His voice echoed hollowly through the room. Not waiting for a reply, he turned off the speakers with the press of a button on the control panel in front of him. "Ladies and gentlemen, it appears we have a rat amongst us."

Ten highly armed guards stormed into the room, surrounding the table. The doors slammed behind them, the lock engaging with a loud click. Suddenly, thick, steel sheets dropped from the ceiling, covering the windows.

The Master's Room had become a prison.

Johanna was the first to her feet. "What is the meaning of this, Dionysus?" she demanded.

Dionysus rose slowly, like it was very painful for him to stand up. "SIT DOWN!" he roared. Dropping his tone a notch, he said, "Or we will make you."

Surprised at the forcefulness of his demand, Johanna eyed one of the guards, who looked ready to make her sit if she didn't cooperate. Reluctantly, she returned to her seat. "Please explain yourself," she asked in a softer tone.

Laughing evilly to himself, Dionysus pointed a finger at the first Council member, who happened to be Andrew, and said, "I have just proven that you are a traitor."

§

Andrew froze.

Dionysus continued, "Or rather, one of you is a traitor." He shifted the aim of his finger casually around the table, pausing on each face, as if to consider it.

Andrew realized he had been holding his breath. He slowly released the air, trying to mask his sigh of relief. Dionysus didn't know it was him. At least not yet.

"The mission that we just listened to—the one that failed miserably because the demons seemed to be one step ahead of us—was only discussed amongst the Council. Even the team involved didn't know what their target was until I personally briefed them on it five minutes before it started. And yet...And yet somehow the demons were ready for us, as they have been on so many occasions. Always one step ahead of us. What is the only feasible explanation for this, my friends? Anyone care to take a stab at it?"

Dionysus's second-in-command, Michael, fearlessly said, "Someone leaked it."

"Exactly. And it had to be someone in this very room, because you were the only ones who knew. We are not leaving this room until the rat, or rats, have come forward and been punished for their crimes." Dionysus smiled. "But first, the rest of the entertainment."

Pressing a button to activate the speakers once more, Dionysus spoke into the microphone. "Lucas, are you ready?"

"Yes, my lord."

"Then let the fun begin."

Forty-One

"I'd say everything went perfectly," Chris countered.

"Listen to me, man. I know these angels. Something is wrong. They are up to something." Sampson had been trying to explain his fears to the demons for fifteen minutes, but couldn't seem to make any headway.

"You may be right, but I think the only thing we can do right now is to leave the lead team here to keep an eye on things, and go back to the Lair to debrief."

Sampson couldn't argue with that. All he had was a feeling, but he couldn't substantiate it and he didn't have any better ideas.

Within seconds, the mission team was back in the teleport room. They charged back down the tunnel. They needed to be ready if there was another attack.

Forty-Two

"Operation Bait and Switch is now underway," Lucas said sharply to his team. As instructed by Dionysus, he narrated their progress for the benefit of the Council, who were plugged into their radio frequency. "Phase one is complete with David Knight having been taken into special custody. We now begin phase two: the capture of Helena and Theodore Knight, and their youngest son, Peter Knight." Lucas grinned, as he pictured the shocked faces of the Council members when they learned the nature of the secret mission. All brought to you by Lucas Sharpe.

His team, hand selected by him for their abilities and trustworthiness, mirrored his delight in being a part of this mission. They huddled around him now. Crab, one of the tougher blokes in the bunch said, "Want me to do the honors?"

"Go for it."

The giant known as Crab leaned back, raising his leg sharply in the air and then smashing the heel of his right boot into the door, shattering the knob, the primary lock, and the deadbolt in one swift motion. Splinters of wood scattered on the tile floor as the door burst open inwards, allowing access to the house. They rushed in professionally, two at a time, covering each other's backs. "We're in," Lucas announced for his audience.

A scream sounded from the next room. "Leave him alone, he's not one of us, he's fragile," said a woman's voice. Lucas strode purposefully into a brightly-lit living room, analyzing the situation. Crab had a terror-stricken man pinned to the wall by his neck. On the couch, a young boy, Peter he presumed, had a gun leveled at his head by another angel. Like his brother, David, the boy had a shocking resemblance to his eldest brother, the infamous Gabriel Knight.

The woman yelling was on her knees, hands clasped tightly together, like she was praying. She continued to beg for the lives of her family. "Please, don't hurt him. He's only a boy." Her thick blond hair fell around her face messily—she had likely been thrown to the ground, rather than ending up there on her own.

A particularly nasty female angel stood over her. She was one of Lucas's favorite recruits. Her name was Cassandra and like Lucas, she had a grudge against Gabriel, having been dumped by him a long time ago or something. Grabbing a fistful of Helena Knight's hair, Cassandra snarled, "Want me to shut her up?"

Beauty and purpose, Lucas thought, admiring the versatility of the blonde bombshell standing before him. "Thank you for the offer, but you will have your chance later. Let me speak to her." Hearing a gasping noise coming from his left, he added, "You can release him now, Crab."

Reluctantly, Crab removed his hand from Theodore Knight's throat. The breathless man fell to the ground, his knees buckling when his feet hit the floor. Crab rested his foot on Gabriel's father's back. "That should hold him, boss."

Lucas turned back to Gabriel's mom. "Don't worry, Mrs. Knight. You and your family might just survive this if you cooperate."

"What do you want from us?" Helena asked angrily.

Lucas strode forward and snapped his hand sharply, like a whip, the back of it connecting forcefully with her face. "Shut up! I'll be asking the questions!"

"Leave her alone," Mr. Knight croaked, his face flush against the carpet. Crab kicked him once, hard in the stomach. Theodore groaned in agony.

"You can shut up, too," Crab grunted.

Cassandra laughed. "This is getting fun already."

"What happened to you, Cassie?" The question came from Helena. "You and Gabriel used to be such good friends."

"Listen, bitch. I'm not the traitor here."

"I...I don't understand. What are you talking about, Cass?"

Lucas said, "Either you are a good liar or you are completely unaware of your eldest son's recent anti-angel activities."

"Gabriel? I haven't heard from him in months. Every time I call they tell me he's on a top-secret assignment."

Lucas licked his lips greedily. He would take especial pleasure in telling her the news. He paused between phrases for effect. "Your son...Gabriel Knight...is a traitor. He tried to help the demons, was sent to prison, broke out, and is now living in the Lair."

She looked genuinely stunned. "That's not possible...I don't believe you."

"I don't really care what you believe. You will believe it soon enough, once we take you back to headquarters. Dionysus can tell you himself if you want. He's the one who authorized this mission. If you're lucky, he'll be merciful. If it were up to me, the family of the traitor would be executed, too." Lucas spat out these last words in disgust.

Helena went to say something, or maybe ask another question, but Lucas beat her to it. "Okay, Cass. Now you can shut her up." A gleam in her eye, Cassandra clamped her hands together and crashed them down on the back of Helena's head, like a sledge hammer. She slumped to the ground, unmoving.

Theodore tried to rise to his feet, but Crab, with lightning quickness, bludgeoned him in the temple with his blaster. The only human in the room rolled twice, and then lay still; a trickle of blood dribbled from his head and began pooling on the floor.

Peter, still sitting on the couch, hugged his knees, his eyes wide with terror. Lucas stood over him. "Don't worry, kid. We won't hurt you, so long as you don't do anything stupid." With a wave of his arm, he motioned for his team to exit the house. They dragged the three prisoners with them.

Once airborne, Lucas announced for his audience: "Mission successful. Gabriel Knight's entire family has been taken into custody. We hope you enjoyed the broadcast. Over and out." Turning off his radio, Lucas breathed in a deep breath of fresh, night air. *If you wiggle a big enough worm, the fish will come*, he thought to himself. And he would take great pleasure in personally filleting Gabriel Knight.

Forty-Three

"Well done, Dionysus. You did it." It was Michael who spoke. Dionysus could tell that his right hand man meant it. He was never really a suspect, but wanted to keep him in the dark just long enough to completely rule him out. Dionysus sighed in satisfaction. He *had* done it. Tricked the traitor, tricked the demons. Now, the trap could finally be set bring Gabriel, and then the girl, back under their control. But first, he had a mole to catch.

"Thank you, Michael." Looking around the room, he asked, "Do you all share Michael's sentiment? That it was a job well done? I know at least one of you is not too happy with the success—bitterly disappointed even. I know at least one of you is trembling inside, sweating from fear of being discovered, kicking yourself for being so careless."

❧

Beneath his white robe, Andrew *was* trembling and he could surely feel the sweat beginning to meander from under his arms and knees. Trying to keep his face steady, he felt like his mouth was contorted unnaturally and that one look from Dionysus would pierce his soul and leave his secrets bare, revealing his treachery. When Dionysus walked past him lazily, he stopped breathing until the shadow had moved on.

❧

Dionysus continued moving around the table. "Duck, duck, duck," he said soothingly, tapping each Archangel on the head gently. "Goose!" he said suddenly, whacking Johanna on the back of her head.

"You think I'm the mole?" She turned her head to glare at him. I have been one of the biggest advocates of The Plan from day one. I may not always agree with your methods, but I have always shared your vision."

"I don't know...," Dionysus mused. "You were pretty quick to demand an explanation for my actions."

"I don't like being held prisoner…and I don't like surprises."

Dionysus considered himself a non-machine version of a lie detector and, in this case, he didn't sense a falsehood. Maybe she wasn't his mole.

※

Andrew's breathing had become shallow, coming and going in short, ragged intervals. He tried to mimic the supremely-confident Michael's position and facial expression—hands folded casually, he looked completely relaxed, radiating innocence from his entire being. Probably because he was. Andrew felt a bead of sweat dribble from his hairline to his eyebrow. Thankfully, it was on the side of his face that Dionysus couldn't see from where he stood.

※

Dionysus moved on from Johanna. Next to her was Sarah. "Hmmm, I've noticed that you always seem to just agree with the popular position, Sarah. That would seem like pretty good cover for a mole, eh? Agree with the majority and then leak our decisions to the enemy, never drawing attention to yourself."

"If you are looking for me to defend myself, I won't. I've been true to this cause since I was born," Sarah said.

Again, the lie detector came up empty. Dionysus had truly believed that the mole was likely to be Johanna or Sarah, or maybe both of them, so for a moment he didn't know how to proceed. Then he remembered the trick up his sleeve: the proof he had asked his technicians to gather; the damning evidence that would smoke out the nasty mole.

"Bring in the report," he ordered, to no one in particular. Someone was apparently listening and heard him, because the locked door clicked open and a short, bald angel entered the room, squeezing through the circle of hefty guardsmen.

"I have it here, sir," he said, handing Dionysus a bound sheaf of papers.

"Thank you. That will be all." As quickly as he had appeared, the bald man exited and the doors were resealed. Sifting the pages of the report through his fingers, Dionysus said, "Over the last week I have had the technicians focused on one task, and one task alone: monitoring any communications in and out of this mountain. While most communications are preauthorized, we have also noticed numerous rogue transmissions. Tracking and pinpointing these transmissions is a difficult business, but our technicians developed an approach that they believe has detected at least 50 percent of these rogue comms. Some they have been able to track to the destination, others from the source, and in a few cases they have even managed to record and transcribe the text.

"In my hands, I have the full report, which I believe will be quite interesting for all of you in this room. This is hot off the press, so even I have not had the pleasure of reading it yet. Let's open it, shall we?"

§

If Andrew was scared before, he was terrified now. He was forced to shove his hands under the table when they began shaking uncontrollably. As his heart raced and the sweat continued to bead on his skin, he desperately tried to think of a way to escape. Fight his way out? With the remainder of the Archangels being loyal to Dionysus, he wouldn't stand a chance, even if he could break through the guards. Lie his way out? He was barely holding it together and was never a very good liar anyway. The only reason he made it this far was because Dionysus never suspected a thing. Suicide? That was a viable solution. He had his light sword under his robe. At least he could die with dignity, rather than sustaining the torture and mockery that Dionysus would surely pour upon his head. His hands no longer shaking, he fingered the sword under the table.

§

Dionysus said, "First page: blah, blah, blah, statistics and such, nothing specific enough to condemn anyone.

Second page: more of the same, skip. Third page. Ahh, now here's something interesting: a single call was made at 3:00 this very morning. Who could possibly need to make a call at such an early hour? Let's read on."

※

The handle felt cold to the touch. His sword hadn't been used in years, as Andrew had lived a double-life within the confines of Mount Olympus. Suddenly, it felt right that he should use it again, after all these years, to take his own life. He was tired of hiding, tired of being scared.

※

"Page four: an in-depth probe into the suspicious call. Apparently the destination could be tracked to somewhere within the demon Lair. Bingo, we've got our mole. Let's see if we can identify the creep. Fifth page: the source of the call was narrowed down to the second quadrant of the Archangels' Quarters. Whose rooms are in the second quadrant?"

Johanna spoke first. "Mine is, but that doesn't prove anything."

"Congratulations, you're still in the running," Dionysus said smartly. "Who else? Don't be shy now."

"Me," a male voice grunted.

"Ahh, Percy. Nice to hear from you. I would never have suspected you of such treachery, but after this I may never trust anyone again." Dionysus leaned over Percy's shoulder and whispered, "Between you and me, I'm hoping it's not you."

※

It was now or never. The next page of the report would link the call to him. Andrew stood up confidently.

"My room is also in quadrant two."

"No need to stand, my dear Andrew. It's all here in the report." Flipping to the next page while Andrew continued to stand, Dionysus said, "Oh my…we are in for a treat. Our genius technicians were actually able to capture a partial recording of the call. Let's hear it, boys!"

The speakers clicked on as if by magic. Andrew's voice sliced through the tension in the room: "They will take her father. Good luck."

All eyes shifted to Andrew, who now had his sword drawn, rays of light shooting up and down the blade. While their attention was drawn to the recording, he had deftly flicked his sword towards Michael; the point was now resting firmly on his neck. Trying to hide the tremors in his voice, he said, "One move by anyone and he dies."

If his sword was aimed at any of the other Archangels, Dionysus would have likely replied, *Go ahead, kill him or her*, but this was different. Michael was like a brother to him and was not replaceable. Andrew, of course, knew this and chose his target wisely. "Let's not do anything hasty, my friend," Dionysus said. "I'm sure we can work something out."

"I am taking him as my hostage and will exchange his life for my free passage from the mountain. Tell the guards to drop their blasters or I'll kill him."

Andrew knew he would never be allowed to leave the mountain, regardless of who his hostage was. He was merely using Michael as a distraction to ensure he could do what he knew he had to do, before he was shot down by the guards' blasters. It would be his final act—one he could be proud of.

"Do as he says," Dionysus ordered. The guards lowered their weapons and dropped them on the floor. "I accept your trade: Michael's life for your freedom. Make way for Andrew," he commanded.

In the ensuing commotion caused by the shuffling guards, Andrew sprang into action, thrusting his sword sharply through Michael's aorta, and then slashing back and forth, severing his head from his neck. Next, before anyone could react or gravity could pull Michael's detached head to the floor, he drove the sword downwards, deep into his own heart. In the few seconds of life that he had left, Andrew could hear the satisfying sound of Dionysus wailing. *If he couldn't kill the evilest*, he thought, *at least he was able to get the second most-evil.* He was at peace, he had done his duty. All went black.

Forty-Four

Chris and Sampson had finished the mission briefing and a round of applause rose from the panel of Elders in appreciation. Taylor was beaming. Her dad was safe. Mission completed.

Once the clapping and whistling had died down, Gabriel said, "Something doesn't smell right here."

"That's what *I* said," Sampson added.

Taylor asked, "What do you mean—that my dad is still in danger?"

Sampson said, "No, I don't think so. The whole thing felt more like a decoy. Like they had something else planned altogether and the attempt on your dad was just a distraction to keep us away from the real target."

Chris interjected: "But you said it yourself, the attackers seemed genuinely surprised that we were there."

Gabriel said, "Yeah, but you don't know Dionysus. In his warped mind, the right hand doesn't always need to know what the left hand is doing. In fact, he may have sent some of his weaker soldiers into what he believed would be a trap, so that he could send his best angels on the real mission."

It was at this point that they noticed Clifford shaking his head strongly. "No, no, no. I strongly disagree. We have a rock-solid source within the angel upper echelon that would have warned us if it was merely a diversion. The source made it very clear where the attack would be."

"I think it's time you revealed the source to us, Clifford," Gabriel suggested.

"The risk is too high," Clifford replied. "It may put his life in danger."

"His life is already in danger! I have worked with Dionysus; I understand his sick brain more than anyone here and it is essential that I know who the source is. The time has come for my people to know the truth about what a monster he is. The days of spying and sneaking around are long past and any who dare to go against Dionysus must be brought into our fold. The demons can be a great asset to us, but the responsibility must now shift to the angels to rise up in full rebellion against the cancer that plagues their race—my race." Gabriel was on his feet now. His face was shining with the confidence and trueness of a man who was born to greatness; there was a fire in his eyes that gave confidence to all those that looked into them. Taylor had seen shades of this fire before, but only a glimmer, a mere glimpse of the potential that was yet to come. She admired his face now, even as she contrasted it to the contorted face of rage and agony he had displayed only a day earlier. The difference was like night and day, light and dark, water and stone.

Silence filled the room, as the Elders marveled at the glowing figure standing before them. Chris whispered to Taylor, "They think he is the leader that has been foretold in legends long past." Taylor looked at him quizzically.

Clifford said, "And will you lead such a rebellion?"

"I will do what is required of me."

Clifford stared off into space as he spoke. "Hmm, yes...yes, I believe you shall. Long have our people foretold that one would rise amongst the angels to lead a great rebellion. Maybe you are that one."

"With all due respect, I am just one. While I may have a part to play, I am not the subject of fairy tales or fantasies, or legends, for that matter."

"No, I guess you're not," Clifford replied tiredly. "In any case, you have convinced me of your need to be aware of our final source within the angels. It is Archangel Andrew."

Both Gabriel's and Sampson's eyes widened and they glanced at each other. "You were able to get to someone within the Archangel Council?" Gabriel asked incredulously.

Clifford said, "Actually, he came to us. You see, he hated The Plan when it first became known to him. But he was one flower amongst a bush of thorns. He came to me in secret and vowed to do whatever he could to help us stop the successful implementation of The Plan. He has been passing us information for a decade. No one would suspect an Archangel of being a spy."

༺༻

Gabriel's brain was in full gear. Trying to think like Dionysus, he considered every potential action that the madman would have considered. Like a computer, he analyzed each backwards and forwards, considering merits, risks, and possible outcomes. The answer appeared. "Oh, no," he breathed.

༺༻

"What are you thinking, Gabriel?" Taylor's eyes had not left Gabriel's face during Clifford's speech. She had seen the surprise, the appreciation, and finally some hidden revelation—some undesirable conclusion. But what?

"We'll be lucky if Andrew makes it through the night," Gabriel said ominously.

"But how....how could he have been discovered?" Clifford asked.

Instead of answering, Gabriel asked a question of his own. "How did he contact you, Clifford?"

"The way he always does—by phone. But he was more cautious than usual. He called late at night, used fewer words—the entire conversation was only ten seconds. He said they would come for Taylor's father. That was it."

Gabriel said, "Dionysus may be evil, delusional, and insane, but he is also smart as hell. A real thinker. They say he meditates for four hours a day and from these marathon brainstorming sessions, most of his strategies are born.

"When the angel spies were discovered and I escaped, he would have launched himself into a rage—throwing things, using his personal assistant as a punching bag, he would have been very destructive. But then, he would have channeled that anger, concentrated it into an intensely focused meditation.

"His paranoia growing, Dionysus would have trusted no one, planning in secret. Gathering information, monitoring communications, searching for his enemies. Given the extent of the treachery that he had already discovered, he might have even assumed that the treachery rose much higher, into his very closest circle. A trap would have been set."

Gabriel's eyes narrowed, and Taylor knew he was zeroing in on his dark conclusion. "What if he purposely allowed the Council to know about the supposed attack on Taylor's father, all the while planning another, more secret mission—the real mission? When his angels walked into a trap at the Kingston's, he would have immediately known that an Archangel had leaked the information. By then, his communications technicians would have gathered sufficient proof to condemn the traitor, while he pulled off another mission."

"But what mission?" Clifford asked.

"We will likely know soon what the real plan was. Dionysus will want to flaunt his victory."

Forty-Five

The demons would have known the nature of Dionysus's true mission almost immediately if not for the disarray that was caused by Andrew's last act of defiance. *Michael was gone.*

Dionysus hoped that Andrew could be revived, but the commitment with which the Archangel had taken his own life was as stalwart as his dedication to his traitorous ways. While Dionysus would greatly miss the opportunity to torture and kill the spy himself, he would simply take it out on Andrew's family, who had apparently gone into hiding. But he wasn't worried, they would be found.

The strength of his pain at the loss of his closest friend and ally was second only to the strength of his desire for revenge. He had mourned Michael's unexpected death for ten excruciating minutes, succumbing to his emotions. Weeping, wailing, and gnashing of teeth seemed like an appropriate description of his torment.

But now, he was refocused on the task at hand. He would dedicate the next year to Michael, although his friend would never bear witness to the beautiful world that he would create. A world of immortality, where angels lived forever and claimed their rightful place of honor as rulers of the earth, where demons had been eradicated like the vermin that they were, and where humans were used as resources—to serve, to reproduce, and to *harvest*.

These were his thoughts as he strode into the holding area; he was flanked by Lucas, who was yammering on about something meaningless. The kid was good, but didn't know when to shut up. When they reached the cell, Dionysus raised a hand to silence him.

The holding area wasn't particularly gloomy or miserable, like the dungeon prison that Gabriel had been confined to, but it was much more pleasant to conduct interrogations in, and prisoners could be tortured just as easily. The cell was stark white and brightly-lit, resembling the padded rooms of a mental institution, but without the padding.

Typically angel prisoners would not be awarded any light, as this would allow them to use their powers, but in this case there was little risk of an eight-year-old and his mom causing any serious damage. Plus, there was a five-foot thick layer of titanium surrounding the cell, through which not even the most powerful angel could escape even if given a hundred years. To ensure her cooperation, all sorts of vile threats had been made on the lives of Helena Knight's husband and child.

"Wait here," Dionysus ordered.

"But, sir, I—"

Dionysus again raised his arm and this time, glared at the *child* beside him. Lucas obediently snapped his mouth shut, tighter than a trap.

Dionysus opened the door and entered the room. Closing the door behind him, he surveyed the occupants, who were watching him with trepidation. The young boy, Peter he remembered, shrank back from him, hiding behind his father. Theodore Knight, who was known as Teddy, thrust an arm across each of his family members, as if to protect them.

Dionysus smiled in amusement. "What are you going to do, human rat? They have a better chance on their own than with you."

"What do you want from us?" Teddy asked.

"In time, all will be revealed. But first, I just want to talk to you, that's all."

"Where is my son?" Helena asked.

"Which one: the traitor, or the dead one?"

A look of horror crossed the parents' faces. "You killed David," Helena said hollowly. It was a statement, not a question.

"Well, not in the classic sense. But he might as well be dead to you, because you will likely never see him again. I will not have you brainwash him like you did Gabriel."

"We never brainwashed anyone," Teddy declared.

"Ideas of rebellion can only be planted in the home," Dionysus instructed wearily, like he had taught this lesson many times before. "It is your fault that your son is a traitor and a fool."

"Anything that he's done, he must have had very good reasons to do," Gabriel's father said fervently. There was pride in his voice.

"Are you going to hurt David?" Helena asked.

"Of course not. He is a very bright young lad—there is great potential in him. We will merely shelter him from your filthy influence. Allow him to realize his full potential."

"You'll never get away with it, this is kidnapping," Helena said through clenched teeth.

"Now I know where Gabriel gets his fighting spirit from, it's surely not from his dad," Dionysus said, chuckling at his own joke. "But yes, we *will* get away with it. Good will prevail."

Dionysus reached into his pocket and extracted a phone. They had searched Andrew's apartment, but the only evidence of treason they had found was the unauthorized "safe" phone. There was only one number programmed into it. Dionysus knew without a doubt whose number it was. Ignoring his *guests*, he flipped open the phone and pressed the call button.

An urgent voice answered before the first ring. "Andrew, you're alive."

"Andrew's dead," Dionysus sneered. He wasn't about to tell him that he had taken his own life or that he took Michael with him.

"Who is this?" Clifford demanded.

"Take a wild guess."

"You evil son of a—"

"Now, now, no need for name calling. Put Gabriel on."

"Why should I do anything that you say?"

"Because if you don't, I'll kill his family," Dionysus said succinctly.

"You're bluffing."

Handing the phone to Helena, he ordered, "State your name."

"Helena Knight," she said into the receiver. Before she could utter another syllable, Dionysus yanked the phone back from her.

"Proof enough?"

"I'll get him," Clifford said bitterly.

Forty-Six

Gabriel was lying on his bed with Taylor. She had been dozing off and on, but he wasn't able to turn his brain off. Some sixth sense told him that his theory was true, that Andrew was probably dead, and that the angels had another plan. As Sampson had said, protecting Taylor's dad had been easy—too easy. What was he missing?

While his mind churned through the events of the last week, there was a forceful knock on the door. "Gabriel, it's Clifford!" a voice shouted.

Taylor awoke with a start, looking groggy. "What was that?" she asked.

"Clifford's at the door," he replied. He sprung out of bed and thrust open the door; he was naked from the waist up and looked like he had just come from the gym, his muscles tensed. He was anticipating bad news of some kind.

Clifford looked defeated. Gabriel braced himself for the worst, but Clifford didn't say a word. Instead, he handed him a phone. Gabriel raised it to his mouth and ear and said, "Hello?"

The voice on the other line was the voice from his darkest dreams, one he hoped he would never have to hear again. And the voice's message was even worse. "Hello, Gabriel. I have your mom. Oh, and your dad, too. And I figured what the heck, so I grabbed your brothers as well."

Rather than fear or sadness, only anger entered his heart. "If you lay one finger on any of them, I swear to God, I will kill you."

"Temper, temper," Dionysus clucked. "Don't you even want proof?"

Gabriel didn't need proof; he knew that this sicko was telling the absolute truth. Regardless, he wanted to hear the voices of his loved ones, if only for a second to know that they were safe. "Yes," he replied simply.

"As you wish," the devil croaked.

There was a moment of static on the line and then, "Gabriel, is that you?"

Instantly recognizing the voice of the woman who had brought him into the world, Gabriel replied, "Yes, Mother. Are you alright?"

"More or less. That brat, Lucas, beat us up a little. Your dad's got a wicked bruise and my neck's a little sore, but other than that, we're just fine. Don't let him use us to—" Her voice cut out.

Dionysus said, "I think that's enough talking for one day. Here's what's going to happen next. You will keep this phone with you at all times. Trust me, Clifford's not going to need it anymore. Soon I will call you with further instructions about how you can save your family. Goodbye, Gabriel."

"Wait!" he roared, but it was too late, the line was dead. He tried to call back on the same number, but the line was busy.

During the conversation, Clifford had leaned in, close enough to hear both sides. Taylor had listened curiously to Gabriel's side of the conversation from the bed. She evidently figured it out from the context.

"They have your family," Taylor stated.

"Yes," Gabriel confirmed numbly.

"Damn angels. We were so worried about my family that we never considered that yours could be in danger, too." Getting out of bed, Taylor tried to comfort him by wrapping her arms around his torso. In a reversal of roles, he shook her off.

"It's not your fault. None of us considered it. Not even me," Gabriel said.

"What do they want?" Taylor asked, once again trying to embrace him.

Allowing her to touch him this time, Gabriel replied, "Me. They want me."

"You can't give yourself to them. They're psychopaths. They'll kill you *and* your family."

"I know, but I have to try."

Previously willing to simply listen, Clifford interrupted: "We will help you. Our full resources will be at your disposal."

Gabriel shook his head. "Thanks, but no thanks, Clifford. If they see me coming with any company, they may start killing people. I'm not willing to take that risk. I have to do this on my own. I'll keep you informed as to my whereabouts through contact with Christopher. If the communications stop, then you'll know I've been taken or killed."

"I'm coming with you," Taylor said.

"Taylor, you know you can't. If the angels get you, it's over."

"But I can help. If you use my aura, you can defeat them all. In the right hands, I can be a weapon for good, right? That's what you once told me."

"Yes, Taylor. But not now, not this way. It is too dangerous. I don't want you with me."

Taylor looked stung, like she'd been slapped in the face. "Fine. Do what you want," Taylor said coldly.

Gabriel knew she was pissed at him. But that was better than putting her life in danger again. Afraid that any delay might cause him to change his mind, Gabriel said, "I will leave immediately. Please tell the rest of my friends what happened, and send Sam to be with Taylor right away."

Taylor said, "I don't need a babysitter."

Gabriel ignored her and looked at Clifford.

"I will. Good luck," Clifford said, putting a hand on Gabriel's shoulder. "And be careful."

Before leaving the room, Gabriel tried to hug Taylor, but she shrank from him, avoiding contact. Gabriel winced, but then said, "I will always love you, Taylor Kingston. And I will come back." His promise was a final lie that he expected to breed hope. When she ignored him, he ran from the room, leaving her alone with Clifford.

Forty-Seven

The boy sat on the bed with his back to the wall, reading a comic book. His initial excitement over having been chosen was wearing off. Now he was just bored. When they had come for him, he was with his friends and he thought they had more questions for him. Ever since his traitor brother had been charged with treason and subsequently escaped, they had asked him a lot of questions. About whether his brother ever told him any secrets, what his mother had taught them as kids, what kind of dad their father was, that sort of stuff. He was tired of answering questions. He was tired of being the brother of the traitor. He was *not* his brother. Not anymore. He hated Gabriel for being a traitor, for being his idol, and for destroying his reputation.

Thus, he was surprised and delighted when Lucas came to speak to him. All the boys were talking about Lucas, the angel that had replaced his brother as the top, young angel talent. He was even more surprised to find out that he had been chosen. Lucas had said, "David, there is talent in your blood and even though your brother chose to use it for evil, we know you will do the right thing." He agreed completely and readily accepted the apprenticeship. After all, he had earned it. Halfway through his second year, he was the top angel in four out of the five mandatory training courses he was enrolled in. For the coming year, he would learn from Lucas, shadow him. Grow his talents.

It was the opportunity of a lifetime, but he was learning that with every opportunity there are drawbacks. He wasn't allowed to see his friends or family while he was an apprentice. And his freedom was limited now that he was confined to the Archangels' Quarters. No one could enter or leave the area without proper security clearance. And he didn't have the clearance. Lucas would need to accompany him almost anywhere outside of the Quarters. But it would be worth it to gain real life experience. He hoped to be an angel in the Special Mission Corps, like Lucas was and like Gabriel had been. So if he had to read a couple of hundred comic books out of sheer boredom, he would do it.

His eyes flicked up when he sensed a presence in his doorway. His eyes widened in shock and he blinked a few times to see if he was imagining things. There at his door was Dionysus himself. "Do you mind if I come in, David?"

Not realizing his lips were even moving, he replied, "Of course, sir. I mean, my lord."

Dionysus stepped across the threshold and admired the room. "Ahh, beautiful in its simplicity," he remarked. "This is a good room. It has a similar look to my room, only mine is a lot bigger," he joked.

David smiled. "I should hope so, my lord."

༶

Dionysus mirrored the boy's smile for a moment and then his face became serious. "I was very glad when I heard that Lucas had selected you as his apprentice." His words were very careful, as he enunciated each and every syllable of *se-lec-ted*. Of course, he was lying, having forced Lucas to take on the boy. It was all part of the mission.

"You...you were?"

"Yes, very. Did Lucas tell you that he's my apprentice?"

"No."

"Well he is. And I guess that makes you my grand-apprentice. I only stopped by to tell you that and to welcome you. Feel free to come to me anytime you would like to talk."

"Wow, thanks, my lord. I will." Dionysus could tell that David felt honored, special, to have been visited by the Head of the Archangel Council.

Without another word, Dionysus turned on his heel and walked rigidly from the room, leaving David to his own thoughts.

Forty-Eight

Clifford had left immediately after Gabriel. It was the middle of the night and Taylor felt exhausted. She lay down to try to sleep, cursing Gabriel's name under her breath over and over again. Eventually she drifted off. When she awoke, she felt around the bed—Gabriel's bed. His bed was empty, except for her. It was still early; something had awakened her. What was it? As she fluffed her pillow, she mulled over this thought. *Something.* Maybe it was a dream, but she couldn't remember now. The room seemed lighter than usual. Located deep within the heart of the mountain, she enjoyed being able to sleep in complete darkness, but now she found herself able to see.

The pillow, the bed, she could even make out the brass handle on the door. What was different?

Looking around the room for the source of the light, she suddenly realized that she was warm, very warm, hot even. She thrust off the covers and nearly screamed at what she saw: her entire body was glowing. It was a subtle glow, but was bright enough to cast a dim lightness on the entire room. She looked…well, she looked like Gabriel.

She had glowed three times previously and all under similar circumstances: when an angel was connecting with her unusually strong aura. As Gabriel had explained it:

"We, as angels, refer to it as your aura. Each human has an aura and, as far as we know, it has always been that way. Your aura is a light that comes from within you. In humans, that light is generally very dim, as opposed to angels, who have extremely bright auras. Because there is such a contrast, we refer to humans as having an 'aura' and angels as having an 'inner light'. Your aura is much stronger than all other humans.

Because angels have the ability to harness the power of light, we are also able to harness the aura of humans. With most humans, however, that aura is so small that the incremental power gained from them is of no real use to us. Even if we were to try to harness the power of a hundred humans, or a thousand, for some reason the power gained is not cumulative. In other words, we can only use the power of the strongest aura amongst the group."

The strongest aura, she thought. Her aura was the strongest, but still, her body had never glowed unless an angel was connecting with her aura. Twice it had been Gabriel and as her body glowed, a wonderful sensation had flooded through her body. Like sunshine on her skin, like a cool breeze through her hair, even like sex in a way, the experience was life-changing. The other time it had been two complete strangers, angel warriors that had used her and abused her. And almost killed her.

Now, as the glow had apparently returned on its own, the sunny-day-cool-breeze-sex feeling returned slowly, creeping from her toes, to her legs, through her stomach, and finally into her head. She smiled in delight. *Ahhh.*

As quickly and unexpectedly as it had come, it was gone. No warm feeling, no glowing. The room was pitch black. *Weird*, she thought. Very weird.

Forty-Nine

"Well, we have to do something!" Chris yelled. He was getting angrier by the second, and was starting to surprise even himself at how reckless he was being with the head of the Eldership of the demons.

Even the usually calm and collected Clifford's blood pressure was up, his face darkening from deep red to dark purple. "And what do you propose we do, Christopher!?" he roared.

Chris took a deep breath. "Look, I'm sorry, but he's our friend. We can't just hang him out to dry. What he's doing is suicide."

"You think I don't know that?"

When Chris found out about the Knights' abduction and Gabriel's decision to try to save them on his own, he called a private meeting with Clifford to voice his concerns. So far, he was getting nowhere.

"I'm going after him," Chris announced stubbornly.

"You will not!" Clifford growled.

"We'll see," Chris said. He rose from his chair and stomped angrily from the room.

Clifford shook his head in frustration. Losing Gabriel would be a major loss, indeed, but losing Chris at the same time would be devastating. They were both born leaders and were exactly who the demons needed to end the War. But he couldn't stop him from leaving, if that's what he wanted to do. He was no dictator.

Fifty

Gabriel felt the warmth of the sunshine on his face, as a light breeze ruffled his hair. It was one of those perfect days—not too hot, not too cold, just right. But he could not enjoy it. In fact, he hated it. The weather should be miserable—cloudy and rainy—to reflect how he was feeling. He felt like he had been punched in the gut. His emotions were torn in more directions than he could fathom.

On one hand he had Taylor, the love of his life, to think about. If he got himself killed she would be devastated. Leaving her was too hard, too painful. On the other hand, his family was depending on him. They would undoubtedly be murdered in cold blood if he didn't do whatever was asked of him. Any attempt to rescue them would result in their deaths. And then there was the third hand, his responsibility to fulfill his destiny, which he couldn't even start to grasp yet. He didn't know whether he was the chosen one that Clifford talked about, but he did feel responsible to tell the angels the truth—the truth about The Plan, the truth about Dionysus, the truth about what their sons and daughters were fighting for. If he tried to save his parents and got himself killed in the process, he would be letting a lot of people down.

He had been sitting on the top of a mountain for hours trying to get his head around these three hands, and which one was the most important. Taylor was certainly important to him personally, but in the scheme of things their love alone wouldn't save the millions of humans that were unknowingly counting on him. His family was clearly important to him as well, but again, saving their lives might be selfish, in a way. He cared not for his own life, if it was lost in an honorable cause. No matter which way he spun things, upside down, inside out, backwards, or frontwards, the conclusion remained unchanged: His number one priority needed to be defeating Dionysus. Even if that meant making sacrifices that he was completely and utterly unprepared to make.

At least that's what his head told him. But his heart was on a completely different page and continued to urge him to try to save his family, and if by some miracle he survived, go back to be with Taylor again. *If by some miracle.* A miracle, that's what it would take. Or destiny, maybe. If destiny, fate, the will of the gods, or just plain dumb luck intervened, perhaps he would see Taylor again.

So here he was, stuck between head and heart, as so many others had been before him, on the literal and figurative precipice of his life. Waiting, waiting. Waiting for what? For a damn phone to ring. For a call from a voice that he wished he would never hear again. From a person who he wished were dead.

The phone rang and his heart skipped a beat.

"Yes?" he answered.

The familiar voice said, "Sundown. Warrior's Plateau. Come alone. Your life for theirs."

"Sounds like the Wild, Wild West, but I'll be there."

"One more thing, the deal only includes those who want to be exchanged."

"What the hell is that supposed to mean?"

"David has decided to remain…with us." The voice was cold, yet jubilant.

"Screw you, he's coming, too, or there's no deal."

"Then they will all die together."

Now was not the time to make demands. He knew that. He would have to find a way to get David out later. "Fine," he agreed. The line went dead.

Gabriel dialed the number he had memorized. Chris picked up on the first ring. "Hello?"

"It's Gabriel."

"I heard what happened. Where are you?"

"Don't worry about that. I'm calling because I promised Clifford I would keep you informed of my progress. I just received a call from the snake himself. I am meeting him on the Warrior's Plateau at sunset to exchange my life for my parents and Peter."

"What about David?"

"He's not coming," Gabriel replied flatly.

"I'm going to help you," Chris said.

"No. You're not. This is merely a courtesy call. No one can come with me or they will kill them all."

"This is suicide, Gabriel."

"I know, but it's the way it has to be."

"Who will lead the other angels?"

"Sampson will. He has purer blood than me anyway. I gotta go, tell Taylor I love her and don't try to help me."

"I'll tell her. You've been a good friend, man. Good luck."

"Thanks," Gabriel said, and then ended the call, afraid his emotions would betray him. He had about five hours to prepare himself mentally for the challenge to come.

Fifty-One

After the excitement of the mission, Sampson and Kiren had found a quiet spot to relax. Despite his concerns about whether Mr. Kingston was the primary target of the angels' attack, Sampson needed a break from conspiracies, strategizing, and war in general. Kiren was easy to talk to, down to earth, for a demon. He didn't feel like he needed to play games with her or show off. He could just be himself. He liked that.

Nestled in a small, deserted cave that he had discovered while exploring the Lair, Sampson put his arm around Kiren and rested his head on one of the pillows they had brought. She tucked her body against his, leaning her head on the crook between his shoulder, arm, and chest. She sighed in contentment.

"Tell me about when you were little," Sampson said.

"Okay. My mom is human and my dad is demon. I am the middle child—my sister is six years older than me and my brother three years younger. My sister, Lira, never wanted to play with me because I was too little. I didn't fit in well at school, so most of the time I ended up playing with my younger brother and his friends. I got along better with boys, so I didn't mind."

"A tomboy, huh? Now that's a shock," Sampson joked.

"Yeah, I could always run just as fast, climb as high, and fight as strong as any of the boys. My sister was different. She played with dolls, used makeup, and liked shopping; she still does.

"As is standard with my kind, when we were five-years-old we learned *what* we were. By then, I had already accidentally started two minor fires. Unlike Lira who hated being a demon, I loved it. I quickly learned to use my powers and dreamed of one day being in the demon army. My mom worried about me and tried to change my mind as to career path. While she loved demons—she married my father even after learning that he was different—she was afraid of losing us at the hand of some 'bloodthirsty angel', as she called them."

"What about your dad?" Sampson asked.

"He had been in the army for twelve years before he met my mom. I desperately wanted his support for my choices and he gave it to me, encouraging me to live the life that would make me the happiest. I am definitely happiest here. Finally, I found a place where I fit in."

"You sure do," Sampson agreed. "I've been meaning to ask, what's with the hair?"

Kiren laughed and raised a hand to touch her short spikes. Under the soft glow from his body he could barely make out the current color: neon red. Kiren said, "I dunno, I guess I just wanted something to make me look brighter. I could just wear colorful clothes but I preferred changing my hair. It's my thing, I guess."

Sampson nodded. Then abruptly he asked, "Could you ever see yourself with an angel?"

"I'm with an angel right now, silly."

"No, I mean, like, *with* with an angel. You know, dating one."

"Wait a minute, Sampson. You're the one who told everyone that we were 'official'. Didn't you mean it?"

"Well, I was sort of joking, and looking to see your reaction. I believe you said, 'I'll think about it.'"

"I was just kidding. Of course I'll go steady with you, Sampson," Kiren joked. Sampson flushed. "Am I embarrassing you, Mr. Tough Angel?"

Recovering quickly, Sampson replied, "No, I'm just not used to dating someone who's tougher than me."

"Aww, you say the sweetest things." Kiren laughed.

"Sorry, I'm not really used to this kind of thing. My next compliment was going to be that you are looking particularly dark today."

"You are doing just fine. And thank you, I am feeling quite dark today. But I'm not sure I believe you. I'm sure you've always had hot angels lining up to get a date with you."

"Trust me, I haven't had a girlfriend in a long time."

"Well, that makes two of us. I haven't had a *girlfriend* in a long time either," Kiren joked.

Sampson was really enjoying Kiren's quick wit. He had always wanted to find someone that he would be able to laugh with, but all of the female angels in the army were completely full of themselves. And he didn't really have a chance to meet many human girls. But with Kiren everything felt so….well, so easy, really.

"Okay, so you've told me about your childhood, how about your time in the Lair?" he asked.

"Enough questions," Kiren replied, leaning her head back and kissing him. Her lips were upside down when they met his.

"A Spiderman kiss," Sampson said, still feeling her breath on his mouth. "I like it." Gaining confidence, he pulled her around to face him and kissed her again, longer and more passionately than the first time. Her hands found his chest and pulled at his shirt.

Sampson was about to succumb to her hands when he heard, "Sampson, Kiren—you in there?" It was Chris.

Wanting to pretend like they weren't hidden in the darkness of the cave, Sampson knew it wouldn't work—the glow of his body in the dark gave him away like a hooker in a Roman cathedral.

"Yeah, we're here. What do you need?" Kiren was kissing his neck now, ignoring the conversation taking place around her.

"We have a situation here. Let's just say you were right. We're holding a special meeting in my room in thirty minutes. Can you guys come?"

"Yep, we'll be there," Sampson managed to murmur before Kiren's lips found his again.

Fifty-Two

Taylor's mind was becoming troublesome. She couldn't seem to think clearly. What with her lover gone on a suicide mission, and her body acting crazy like it had a mind of its own, she didn't know what emotion was appropriate for the situation.

After waking up to the sight of her strange, glowing body, she knew there would be no way she would be able to sleep. Eventually, she left her room in search of Chris. She wanted to tell him what had happened. Maybe he would know what to do.

No one answered when she knocked on his door, so she went for a walk. Subconsciously, she ended up on a transporter headed for the gargoyle dungeons. When she arrived, she couldn't get through the security door, so she sat down to wait for someone to come along. Shortly after six in the morning, the gargoyle master approached her.

"Access to this area is for authorized personnel only," he said, before recognizing her. "Hey, wait a minute. Aren't you that human girl?"

She stuck out her hand. "Taylor Kingston."

"Name's Barnaby, but most everyone calls me Gargo," he said, taking her hand. Gargo may have been a good looking guy at some point in his life, and maybe he still was, but it was impossible to tell now. His thick, black hair was long, easily reaching past his shoulders, and covering his eyes and ears. A bushy beard and untrimmed mustache potentially hid entire colonies of bats, rats, and insects. His dirty tank-top highlighted a rock-hard physique though—he looked much stronger than Gabriel or Chris—which was probably the result of all his work with the gargoyles. With a twinkle in his eye and a warm smile, Taylor liked him immediately.

"Would you mind if I say hello to a friend of mine, Gargo?"

"I've heard about your connection with the newest member of my flock. It's quite remarkable actually. I've never seen one of them take to someone so much. You can feed him for me if you like." The grizzly bear of a man opened the steel door and held it for Taylor.

"Great, thanks." Like before, Rocky's head was poking out of the cage and he was making squealing sounds, almost like a pig playing in mud, well before she had even crossed half the distance to him.

"Hey, buddy," Taylor exclaimed. "Miss me?" More squeals of excitement. "I'll take that as a yes."

As she reached down to stroke the crown of his head, Taylor said, "Wow, I would swear he grew a foot from yesterday!"

"Yeah, they grow up fast." He grabbed a tape measure from a nearby supply stand and used it to test her statement. "Good guess. He's up ten inches on the dot from yesterday. That is actually well above the average growth rates for newborns. He may turn out to be a big one. You know where the food is?"

"Yeah, but I'm not sure how much to feed him."

"Easy. I prepare everything the night before, just look for the tray in the fridge marked 'Rocky'. At this age, it's almost impossible to over-feed them." Taylor followed his instructions and brought the plate out for her scaly friend, using heavy duty oven mitts like Chris had shown her before. Given Rocky's appreciation for cooked food, she couldn't be too careful. Today he was in the mood for medium rare, using only a quick burst of fire to sear the meat. Apparently he had honed his method overnight. He was as smart as he was friendly.

"Amazing," Gargo said. "Never seen one of them do that either. He's a special one alright."

Taylor spent the next hour feeding, petting, talking to, and teaching tricks to Gargo. When she was done with him, he had learned to stand on one leg, roll over, and play dead. Essentially, he could easily mimic anything that she demonstrated for him. It was great fun and by the time Gargo had finished his morning work, Taylor had completely forgotten about Gabriel and her glowing body. "Thanks, Gargo. That was exactly what I needed this morning."

"Anytime, Taylor. Take care."

She let herself out and waited patiently for the next transporter. When the shiny, metal doors opened, she was surprised to see Chris's unsmiling face. He was the only passenger and did not look happy.

"Quick! Get in, Tay. I've been looking for you." Taylor cringed as she guessed that her carefree morning was about to end. *Back to reality*, she thought.

Fifty-Three

He knew there was no time to spare—restrictions on teleporting could be ignored. Chris grabbed Taylor's hand as soon as she boarded the transporter, and teleported them both back to his room, where Sam, Sampson, and Kiren were already waiting. Taylor silently took a seat next to Sam.

"Unauthorized teleporting, shame on you," Kiren joked.

"Trust me, it is warranted under the circumstances," Chris replied.

"What circumstances?" Sampson asked. "You said that I was right about something?"

"Yes, you were."

"Shouldn't we wait for Gabriel?" Sam interjected.

"He's gone," Taylor whispered. "That's what this is all about."

"Taylor, do you want to tell them since you were the first to find out, or should I?" Chris asked.

She spoke slowly, in clipped sentences, like she was reading blurbs on a newswire. "Clifford came to our room. There was a phone call for Gabriel. It was Dionysus. He has Gabriel's family. He went to rescue them. He doesn't want our help. That's it."

"I have more news," Chris said.

Taylor's somber face suddenly came alive with interest. "Where is he?"

"He wouldn't tell me where he is. Just that he would be meeting Dionysus on the Warrior's Plateau at sunset. He is going to trade himself for his family." Chris purposely omitted that David would not be included in the trade. He didn't want to speculate on the reasons. They would have to deal with that issue separately, when the time was right.

"Oh God," Sam said.

"What's the Warrior's Plateau?" Taylor asked rigidly, without a trace of emotion in her voice.

Chris explained: "Years ago, the War included scheduled battles of each side's strongest hand-to-hand combat warriors. The fights took place on the Warrior's Plateau, which is a flat, rock outcropping located a couple of miles east of the main battlefield. As far as I know, the area has not been used for anything for decades."

"Why meet there?" Sam asked.

"I dunno. A neutral place. Tradition. Random choice. Who knows?" Chris replied.

"What are we going to do to help Gabriel?" Sampson asked.

Chris desperately wanted to voice his opinions, but wanted to let the rest of them come to the same conclusion on their own. "He specifically said that no one should come. He's worried that if we make an appearance, they will kill his family immediately."

"And lose their only leverage? Not a chance," Sampson said. "If we show up, they will try to escape with his family, so that they don't lose their advantage."

Kiren added, "We can't just sit by and let him be taken. They'll kill him. And they probably won't release his family anyway."

"I'm coming," Taylor declared.

All eyes went to Taylor. Sam held her hand. Looking at her intently, Chris said, "I'm not sure that is such a good idea. It might distract Gabriel because he will be worried about your safety, and even if he or Sampson can connect with your aura, I don't think it will be that effective for close-range combat. I would worry that one of us might be killed by it."

"This is not debatable," Taylor replied firmly. "He's my boyfriend and I am tired of him being thrown into deadly situations and me being told that I can't help him. It worked last time, didn't it?"

Chris couldn't argue with that. Taylor's bravery had saved them all the last time. "Okay," he said simply.

"Okay?" Taylor confirmed. He nodded.

"She might actually distract Dionysus more than Gabriel," Sampson said. "I think we can use that to our advantage."

"True. I had a whole plan worked up, but everything changes with Taylor's presence. Anyone have any ideas?" Chris asked.

"It's all about the element of surprise," Sampson said. "They'll be expecting just Gabriel, for all the same reasons that he instructed us not to come. And even if they expect him to have backup, they most certainly will not expect Taylor to be there. Here's what I propose…"

Over the next half-hour, Sampson walked them through his idea, and they diagrammed and practiced it until everyone involved understood it backwards and forwards. It was beautiful in its simplicity. Essentially, they hoped it would go down like this: Chris would teleport in with Taylor, causing a major distraction to both Gabriel and Dionysus. When either Gabriel or one of the enemy angels got close to Taylor, Chris would teleport them somewhere else on the Plateau. Amidst the confusion, Kiren would teleport Sampson into the fray, as near as possible to Gabriel's family, attempting to free them and escape. Chris would then try to escape with Taylor and Gabriel in tow.

The team also discussed contingency plans for every possible scenario, including Taylor's or Gabriel's capture, or the death of one of the team members. The conversation was professional in nature, but all the talk of death and abductions would undoubtedly be hard for an outsider to take.

"And I just sit here alone by myself, hoping that my boyfriend, best friend, and other friends come home in one piece?" said Sam. She sounded frustrated.

Chris had forgotten about Sam, who would play no role in the mission; she had been listening quietly the whole time. He hugged her gently now. "I'm sorry, babe. You probably have the hardest job of all: waiting."

"Are you sure I can't come along for the ride. Just to watch, of course." She said it with a smirk, knowing full well that Chris would never go for it.

"Maybe next time, babe."

"It's okay, I'll be fine. I'll just play pool by myself, or pig out on comfort foods at the café, or maybe make friends with a gargoyle like Taylor did."

Sam's joking had lightened the mood and everyone was smiling now. "We will *all* make it back," Taylor promised.

"I know you will. I'm just being a pain."

"At least you're a funny pain," Taylor said.

"Thanks. How long do you all have before you need to leave?"

Chris said, "It's still a few hours before dusk. We should do something fun."

At the prospect of enjoying some time with her friends before their potentially deadly mission, Sam's face brightened considerably. "Let's go," she said.

"One final thing," Chris added, "no one can breathe a word of this to anyone. Clifford is very against it and might try to stop us from going."

They all agreed to keep the mission a secret. Chris wondered if he was making a big mistake.

PART IV

"You say you wander your own land
But when I think about it
I don't see how you can
You're aching, you're breaking
And I can see the pain in your eyes
Says everybody's changing
And I don't know why

So little time
Try to understand that I'm
Trying to make a move just to stay in the game
I try to stay awake and remember my name
But everybody's changing
And I don't feel the same

You're gone from here
And soon you will disappear
Fading into beautiful light
Cause everybody's changing
And I don't feel right"

Keane- "Everybody's Changing"
From the album *Hope and Fears (2003)*

Fifty-Four

"You have so much to learn, David, but we see great potential in you." Lucas grinned at the boy as they walked; he appeared fatherly, with his arm around David's shoulders.

"I will try my best, sir." David was clearly excited about his first opportunity to go on a mission with his master, but also seemed a bit nervous.

"This will be your first test, David. Are you up to it?"

"I think so, master."

"Good."

They walked into the Master's Room, where the Council was already assembled. Unlike the last time Lucas had been in this room, when all he could feel was power and honor within these four walls, there was an obvious strangeness in the air. It was tangible, like you could almost see it, or smell it, or taste it. Strangely, it felt like the two missing Archangels created a larger presence dead than they did alive. Their impact was palpable. No one dared to sit in the empty seats vacated by their passing.

The Council had already been briefed on David's role in the mission and they approved of the mind games for which he would be used. They not only wanted to kill Gabriel physically, but also destroy him mentally and emotionally. He needed to pay for his treason.

ෆ

David was the only one who didn't recognize the difference in the room. He tried to look proud with his head held high, but he could feel his legs shaking, his heart pumping—his hands were clammy. He took a seat next to Lucas.

Initially, David just stared down at his hands, but eventually gathered up enough courage to peek up at the faces around the table. Some were just staring at him, but most were smiling. The most animated smile of all belonged to Dionysus. When David's eyes locked on his, Dionysus nodded at him encouragingly. After that, David felt much more comfortable.

"First, I would like to thank our guests of honor, Lucas, and his newly acquired apprentice, David Knight." It felt weird for David to hear his name spoken in such a formal setting, and couldn't help but to smile with pride. "Both of them will also be participating in the mission later today, so I thought it wise to include them in this strategy session. Are there any questions before we begin?"

Johanna stood up. "Given the treachery within this boy's family, I think we would all gain some comfort from hearing him speak."

"I have already deemed him to be honorable and trustworthy," Dionysus replied.

"Even so, I think the majority of us would like to hear it straight from the horse's mouth, if you'll excuse the expression."

"Any objections to this?" No hands went up. "Fine. David, will you tell the Council what your feelings are towards the demons?"

When the question was asked, David was gazing at the ornately carved ceiling. Intricate designs of brutal battles showing angels beheading, maiming, and killing demons filled the whole of the ceiling. He didn't realize they were talking about him until the question had already been asked. When he saw everyone staring at him, he stammered, "Wha…What?"

"My young boy. I know this is a lot for you to take in. But if you would be so kind as to give the Council your opinion of demons, we can move on."

He was happy to get such an easy question. "Demons? I hate 'em."

Dionysus smiled, clearly pleased by the response. "And what about traitors to the angels, like the spies that were brought to justice?"

"They are filth, scum. They deserve to be executed."

Still smiling, Dionysus took it a step further: "How about your brother, Gabriel?"

"I hate him the most," David answered simply. There was no lie to detect.

"Satisfied?" Dionysus asked.

"Yes," Johanna said. The other Archangels nodded or simply said nothing. David's face was as hard as stone, his brows furrowed into an angry frown, his lips pursed. All he could feel was anger at the thought of Gabriel. How dare he abandon his own kind? How dare he abandon him?

"Now, if there are no other questions, we shall proceed with the mission strategy session." Staring directly at David, he said, "The purpose of this mission is to apprehend or kill the fugitive, Gabriel Knight."

David's mouth went dry and his head started spinning. *Yes*, he hated his brother, but he still had a child's hope that he would return, that he would change his mind and come back for him. He didn't want him dead. Somehow, he kept his face firm, not a trace of emotion betraying him.

"And we will use Helena, Theodore, and Peter Knight as bait!" The words seemed to echo off of everything in the room—the four walls, ceiling, floor, tables, chairs, and people. David felt the words vibrating through his head and he couldn't help but to blurt out, "But you can't do that!"

All eyes were on him now, causing his face to turn as red as a beet and his knees to knock firmly together.

Lucas said, "Do you trust me, David?" David nodded cautiously. "Look, your brother has done some really bad stuff, right?" He nodded again. "And he needs to be brought back here, so he can't cause any trouble, don't you think?" More nodding. "The only way we can get him to come to us, is by using your family. We won't hurt them if they cooperate, and we won't even hurt Gabriel, as long as he doesn't do anything stupid. All we want is to get him back where he belongs and see if he can be rehabilitated."

David puzzled over Lucas's words for a moment. "Rehabilitated?" he asked slowly, sounding out the word.

"Yeah. You know, fixed. His mind is very broken right now. He doesn't know right from wrong any more than he knows good from evil, or black from white. If we can just reason with him, make him see the light, maybe, just maybe, we can talk some sense into him. And then you'll have your brother back. Would you be able to help with that, David?"

"Um, yeah, I could definitely do that. And you won't do anything to my family?"

"Of course not, David. They volunteered to help bring your brother back in." This time it was Dionysus that spoke. His soft, black eyes looked kind, caring.

"They did?" David asked.

"Yes, of course." Dionysus paused. "Now back to the mission." David barely heard a word that was said the rest of the briefing. Despite their reassurances, David's heart still yammered within him, like a hammer pounding away on his internal organs. He caught something about every Archangel doing their part and being part of the mission, and how Lucas would be responsible for grabbing Gabriel when he was close enough.

"And you, David," Dionysus said, once again making eye contact with him, "will need to help us convince Gabriel of the error in his ways, to turn himself in and cooperate. This will be a very important and difficult task. Gabriel will try to brainwash you, son. He will tell you evil lies to try to convince you to be a traitor, too, but you must resist him. Can you do it, David? Can you do it for your brother?"

David's head suddenly felt clear, like he finally had purpose in his life—to help his brother. Gabriel had done so much for him over his life and he would now have the chance to do something for Gabriel. His brother's head was just confused, he needed help. And David would be the one to provide it.

"Yes, my lord," he replied. "I'll do whatever it takes."

"Thank you for your service. You are learning so quickly. I am proud of you, David."

At this, David beamed. He would follow in his brother's footsteps by becoming respected in the angel army, but he would also learn from his mistakes. He would *not* become him. He would be his own man, like Gabriel had always taught him.

Fifty-Five

Gabriel was hiking. While not a particularly unusual activity for a human, for an angel it was remarkably strange. Why hike in the wilderness when you could fly? But he needed something to help clear his head, to focus him. The exertion helped.

After his phone call with Chris, he had flown to the base of a small, moderately-steep mountain, and then started to hike up it. By three o'clock, he was drenched in sweat from the effort. His shirt was off and slung over his shoulder, used now only as a towel to mop the beads of salty liquid from his face. The muscles in his legs were sore from the climb, and although they would recover much quicker than a human's would, he still needed to rest.

After successfully traversing a particularly steep stretch of large boulders, Gabriel paused on a natural rock ledge to catch his breath. It was then that he realized how hungry he was—his abdomen ached, as the muscles contracted around his empty stomach. Thankfully, he had planned ahead somewhat, packing a small bag with a shoulder strap for necessities, like food and water. Unclasping the bag, he extracted a canteen and drank deeply, emptying more than half of his supply. Next, he munched on a granola bar, some raisins, and a bag of chips. It wasn't particularly satisfying, like a nice lunch in the demon café would have been, but it stopped his stomach from hurting.

Now he had a decision to make. Continue his march up the mountain until it was time to meet Dionysus, or rest up so that he was in peak shape for the confrontation. Either way, he needed to come up with a plan of attack—or a plan of submissiveness.

Pondering the question, Gabriel gazed down at where he had hiked from. The unspoiled landscape was beautiful and he felt his breath catch for a moment, as he appreciated the natural beauty of the world. The colors of Mother Nature's palette caught his attention like never before. The greens of the leaves on the trees and plants seemed greener. The blues, purples and reds of the flowers blooming seemed more colorful, more vibrant.

He spotted a cardinal, sitting high on a tree branch with not a care in the world. Gabriel could fly, but he was no bird. Birds were free, their lives were simple. Hunt for food, find a mate, procreate, protect your young, and then do it all again. The middle was filled with flying— playing with your friends on the gusts of wind that preceded a storm. And singing simple, yet beautiful melodies to all those lucky enough to hear them. *If only*, he thought. His life was anything but free. In a figurative sense he was in a cage, trapped by the impenetrable walls of responsibility that surrounded him.

His thoughts turned to his family. In the depths of his soul he could hear their desperate cries for help. *Save us, Gabriel!* But that was just his imagination. Helena was far too proud to plead for *her* life. For the lives of her family, sure, but not for hers. She would take her chances and keep her head held high. And his father, while a human, had the heart of a lion. He would give his life to save even a stranger. He couldn't allow these wonderful people to be harmed!

If he gave himself willingly, with no struggle, would Dionysus really release them? There was certainly no guarantee. Dionysus would probably just take all of the Knights into custody: one big family reunion.

The hike having refreshed and focused him, Gabriel's mind started to make the connections quickly, taking a similar path to the one that Sampson had earlier that day.

They won't release my family, regardless of whether I cooperate. That much was clear to him now. But if he fought back, wouldn't they kill his family immediately? *Not likely, because then they wouldn't have anything to bargain with.* It was he who Dionysus was after, not his family. On the other hand, they might kill *one* of his family members—make an example of one of them to prove to him that they were not bluffing, that they were serious. That way, they would still have their bait, *and* force him to cooperate. What would he do if they killed Peter, say, or Teddy, or heaven forbid, his mother? They could do it right in front of him, while he was fighting to protect them.

"What *would* I do?" he said aloud, trying to get his mind around the question. Something told him that the answer to this question was of the utmost importance, but for some reason he couldn't seem to think straight. It was like taking a test and suddenly going blank, or going to the store and forgetting what you wanted to buy. He slapped himself hard in the face to try to snap himself out of his stupor.

"ARGHHHH!" he roared at the top of his lungs. *Breathe*, just breathe. *Calm down*, he thought. Try another technique. Like..............what?

Just think about something else and maybe the answer will come to you. He remembered his dad telling him this once when he was upset as a young boy. One of his favorite toys was missing and he remembered playing with it, but not where he had put it afterwards. It was a Nerf Turbo football, he remembered now. His dad had said, "Son, sometimes your mind just needs to be distracted. So go somewhere else and just think about something else and maybe the answer will come to you."

At the time he thought it ridiculous. How could thinking about something else make you think about what you wanted to think of in the first place? Even the question sounded crazy. But he listened to his wise father and went to watch TV. There he was, being blitzed by colorful, manic advertisements about why he should buy the newest Super Soaker water gun and how much fun the rides were at Geronimo Amusement Park. That's when it hit him. He knew exactly where that darn football was. As clear as day, he could remember bringing it back in the house, taking it up the stairs, and kicking it into the closet. It was not a place he would normally store it, but for some reason he did. *And he remembered.*

Now, with no other choice, Gabriel decided to try to employ the same technique to figure out the answer to his question, to know with a certainty what he would do if someone from his family were killed in front of him. He still didn't fully understand why this question felt so important, but he trusted that his instincts were guiding him to some vital truth.

Gabriel turned his mind to the other most important person in his life—Taylor. If he closed his eyes and thought about it hard enough, he could almost feel her hand on his back, her lips on his own—he could even detect the smell of her hair. While he would die for his family in a second if he had to, it would be a great sacrifice indeed. He would not just be giving up his life, but rather, he would be giving up his life *with her*.

And they had the chance for a real future together. A future filled with love and joy and family and friends and laughter. A good life. A life worth living.

Even as Gabriel tried to picture how his life would be after the War was won and Dionysus was defeated, his mind released the information he had been seeking. *He would fight.* If Dionysus killed someone in his family, he would not cooperate, he would fight. Pain, hatred, honor, strength: He could feel it searing through him, piercing him to the core of his existence. He would not go quietly and trade himself for his family. Gabriel Knight would not only rescue his family, but he would rescue himself. He would live!

Immediately, he knew that it was not selfishness that led him to this decision. Of course, he wanted a life with Taylor more than anything, but that's not what drove his decision to fight. Somewhere within his skull a decision was made that defied all logic, which on the face of it appeared to be reckless and dangerous, but which he somehow knew was the right decision. He knew this without a doubt in his mind, by some leadership instinct he had been blessed with.

It was time to find a place to wait that was a bit closer to the action.

Fifty-Six

"Nice shot, Taylor," Sam said sarcastically.

"Damn," Taylor said. The white cue ball had jumped off the table and nearly drilled Chris in the knee.

Chris retrieved the ball and handed it back to Taylor. "You know, jumping the ball is actually a pretty advanced technique, Taylor. I'm impressed," Chris joked.

"Yeah, but I think it's supposed to stay on the table," Taylor mused.

Taylor was trying to laugh and have fun with her friends, but the dark thoughts in the back of her mind kept creeping out, pressing their icy fingers and toes into the front of her mind. Gabriel was out there all alone.

There was no one to hold him or to tell him that everything would be okay. Sure, he was tough and macho and brave and all of those very impressive things that she loved about him, but that didn't mean that he didn't need support.

If only he wasn't so damn stubborn, she thought. She could have gone with him, even if only to keep him company until the meeting. But then she wouldn't be going on the mission to save him. Maybe it was better that she hadn't gone with him. *Maybe it was better this way*, she thought. Surprising him. Not like "Surprise! Happy Birthday!" More like "Surprise! Let's kill an Archangel, save your family, not die, and get the hell out of here!" Taylor laughed out loud at her thoughts.

"That's the first real laugh I've heard from you all day, Tay," Samantha noted. "I didn't think my shot was bad enough to laugh at."

Taylor looked at Sam blankly. Lost in her thoughts, she had forgotten they were playing pool. "What? I wasn't laughing at your shot."

"I know you weren't, I was just kidding. I could tell you were a million miles away. Thinking about him?"

"Sort of."

"Don't worry, you'll save him."

Taylor flinched, startled by her friend's remark. She had expected her to say, "The guys will save him," or "Chris will get him out."

"How could I save him?" Taylor asked. She waited for a sign. Maybe Samantha had a vision in a dream or Taylor's face had appeared to her in the gravy on her mashed potatoes at lunch. She got neither.

"I don't know. I'm not sure why I said that. It just felt like the right thing to say."

Taylor nodded, not understanding at all. After all, she would merely be a decoy in whatever transpired later that day. It was possible that her presence would be one of the many factors leading to the successful completion of the mission, but surely she would not be ultimately responsible for saving Gabriel's life.

Sampson and Kiren entered the room, returning with five drinks.

Suddenly, Taylor felt the tingling in her toes. Panicking, she said, "Uh, I gotta go to the bathroom. Kiren, play for me?"

"Sure, Tay."

"Is everything alright? Do you want me to go with you?" Sam asked.

"I don't need an escort to the bathroom like some high-heeled, drunk off her ass chick. I'll be right back." Taylor hoped she had kept an honest face and that her voice wasn't too shaky. She was so focused on the warm sensation—which had moved up her legs—to tell what she was saying or how she was sounding. Luckily, the rec room had a bathroom.

All the stalls were empty and she was barely able to stumble into one and latch the door before the tingling had covered her from head to toe. "Wow," she panted. It felt like all the good emotions in life had been torn up and scattered throughout her body, like confetti, covering every inch, every fiber. Even her freckles could feel it. Laughter, happiness, love, attraction, friendship, kindness, goodness, physical contact, eating, sleeping—the gamut of emotions and pleasant feelings far exceeded what her mortal brain was able to comprehend. But she didn't care, it felt wonderful.

Then the glowing began. Like the night before, she radiated light seemingly from within her, like her aura was saying hello to the world, or trying to get out of her, or something. *Or something.* Her mind immediately guessed the worst. What if she was dying and had cancer or some rare disease usually found only in monkeys? Or maybe she was just becoming a human light bulb, and would be studied by scientists for the rest of her life, while residing in a perfectly livable, perfectly round plastic bubble.

Taylor realized she was laughing hysterically—partially because of her crazy thoughts, and partially because of how good she felt. Thankfully, no one had come into the bathroom yet, or she would likely have been dragged out and committed to a place with much softer walls than she was used to.

"Get a hold of yourself," she said, still laughing through gritted teeth.

As quickly as it had come on, the feeling passed. Her inner glow worm was switched off, and she was just normal, unglowing Taylor again. Well, as normal as the human girl with the most powerful aura in the world could be, anyway. "Whew," she breathed, still trying to catch her breath from all the laughing. "What is happening to me?" she asked out loud. No one answered. *That was good*, she thought. At least she wasn't hearing voices…yet.

As she staggered out of the stall, she wondered whether she should tell someone what was happening to her. If she had to tell someone, she would rather it be Gabriel. It would have to be later though, once Gabriel was safe again. Looking at her face in the mirror, she looked refreshed, the dark circles under her eyes from the previous night's lack of sleep having mysteriously disappeared. The makeover was miraculous. She remembered looking at herself in the mirror in Chris's bathroom and seeing a tired, rundown, distraught girl. Now, she looked like herself again. No…It was more than that…She looked like a *better* version of herself.

Afraid of all the questions she would get from Sam if she delayed much longer, Taylor left the bathroom to rejoin her friends.

ഉ

"Sorry, Tay. I lost," Kiren said, handling the pool stick back to Taylor as she approached.

"Damn."

"What took you so long?" Sam hissed in her ear. Despite the fact that Taylor didn't linger very long in the ladies room—she couldn't have been in there for more than five minutes—Sam knew her friend too well. Taylor was always very quick in the bathroom. As a rule, she never preened, primped, applied make up, vomited her lunch into the toilet, or stared at herself in the mirror.

"I had to go number two," she said bluntly.

Samantha eyed her friend suspiciously. "Right, if you say so. Well, you do look a lot better. You looked like death before."

"Thanks," Taylor said sarcastically.

"Well, you did."

"Glad to know I'm looking closer to life now," Taylor joked.

Sam smiled. "I was worried about you. Still am."

"Don't worry. Like you said, I'll save Gabriel. And then I'll come home and whip your butt in pool."

"If that happened, then I would know for sure that the world was ending!" Sam laughed.

They resumed their game of pool, playing four at a time with the fifth player rotating in after each game was over.

They were just killing time.

There was just one hour to go before the mission.

Fifty-Seven

After the strategy session, Lucas knew he needed to spend some time with David. He had seen the boy's face when he heard the nature of the mission, and while they seemed like they were able to convince him to support the cause, he was still concerned that David would change his mind in the heat of the moment. Unlocking his apartment door, he said, "This is my place, David."

He pushed the door open and the boy cried out with glee upon seeing the size of the space. Relative to his own room it was massive, at more than 2,500 square feet. Complete with marble floors, brilliantly lit walls and ceilings, and brand new leather furniture, the apartment was big enough to house an entire family.

"You've got an LED!" David exclaimed, running over to the razor-thin widescreen television mounted on the wall. "Awesome! What is it, 50-inch?"

"Yep," Lucas confirmed. "You like electronics?"

"Of course," David replied, making the question sound stupid, like everyone in the world loved electronics more than anything. In truth, David was an electronics junkie. Growing up, he had constantly asked, begged, and pleaded with his parents to get him whatever the newest thing was. Lucas knew this, of course.

"So you get all of this because you are the leader of the Special Missions Corps?" David asked.

"Yes, David. Dionysus is a very kind and generous man. He knows that I am out there risking my neck every day and so, he grants me a few luxuries. This is my sanctuary when I'm not working."

David stared at the LED in silence. Lucas could tell there was something he wanted to ask. "What is it, David?"

"It's just...I was just curious. Would Gabriel have lived here before you?"

Lucas smiled. "Yes, he had this space before me, although I've made a few improvements since he...*left*. He would still be here if he hadn't—"

"If he hadn't been a traitor," David finished.

"Well, yeah, to put it bluntly. Your brother had it all, David. He would have been a star. Hell, he was already a star. Don't make the same mistakes he did."

"I won't," David said firmly.

"Gabriel probably would have said the same thing when he was your age, but look what happened. It's not as easy as you think, David. Your brother, the demons—they will tell you anything to get you change sides. You have to be ready for their lies. You cannot trust anything Gabriel says to you. Not until after we have tried to cure him."

David's eyes brightened. "Do you really think there's hope that Gabriel can be rehabilitated?" he asked, using the word he heard during the meeting.

Lucas's eyes became misty. He was quickly learning how to act from Dionysus, the master himself. "There is always hope, David, but I don't want to raise your expectations. With Gabriel I think it is a long shot. The last time I saw him he tried to kill me. His mind is very far gone."

"Well, I will do what I can to help him," David promised solemnly.

"Thank you. Maybe one day Gabriel will also be able to thank you for it." Lucas was impressed with how fast he had been able to turn the boy completely against his brother; David now seemed to believe that Gabriel was a raving lunatic that required immediate psychiatric attention. Now for the even bigger challenge: to turn him against his family. He paused to collect his thoughts.

Starting slowly, he said, "I have something else to tell you, David."

David looked up at him expectantly.

"What the Council told you about your family wasn't entirely true." He let this sink in.

David asked, "Why would they lie to me?"

"Well, even though Dionysus and I trust you completely, there are some on the Council that are concerned that you are not a true-blue angel and could be turned, just like your brother. They thought it best to hide some details from you, so that you wouldn't try to leak the information to the demons."

"I would never do that," David said fiercely.

"Oh, I know that, David. Believe me, I do. But others are not convinced."

"I will prove it to them. I promise, I will."

"Good to hear. Now, the thing about your family. We told you that they volunteered to act as bait to lure Gabriel closer to us, right?" David nodded once. "Well, they did volunteer, but their motives were slightly different. We think they have been turned by the demons, too, and they are just trying to reunite with Gabriel. You know, become part of his rogue squad."

David felt like he had been slapped in the face. Stunned, devastated, his entire world crashing down upon him. First, the one he had looked up to since he was a little boy, and now his parents were traitors, too? Had the entire world gone mad? His shoulders slumped, his head dropped.

Lucas said, "I'm sorry, David. I know this is hard to take, but I needed to prepare you for the lies that they would try to feed you. It is going to be a hard day for you, but I will be there with you every step of the way."

David felt like crying, but didn't want to show any signs of weakness in front of his master. Instead, he turned the pain, the anguish, the shock, and the devastation into fuel. *Determination.* More than anything, he wanted to prove to everyone that he was better than those who had raised him, those who he had trusted. He had to be better. Someone had to honor the family name. It was his calling.

"I am up for it." His bitter face had morphed into determination that was bred from anger. Fierce, fierce, fiery, hot anger. Life changing anger.

"I know you are, David. Today is your chance to prove to the Council that you are worthy of their trust. I believe that by the end of the day you will have surpassed your peers in every possible category, and will be ready to join the Special Missions Corps a year earlier than what is typically permitted."

"You mean I could join as a 17-year-old?"

"Yes, immediately following your apprenticeship, in a few years. If you are ready, that is?"

"I would be honored," David said calmly, trying to hide his true emotions. Inside he was turning cartwheels, but controlling his emotions was all part of growing up and he needed to learn to do it.

"Good. Do you have any other questions?"

"I don't think so. Only, what do we do now?"

"All I want you to do is go back to your room and prepare yourself mentally for the task ahead. That means meditation in complete silence. No comic books or music. You have less than an hour to prepare; I'll collect you when it's time."

"Yes, master," David said obediently.

He started to leave, but Lucas grabbed his arm. "One more thing, David. We have a special mission for you today. We'll tell you before we leave. Will you do it?"

"Anything you wish, master."

"Good."

Upon leaving the room, he walked casually down the hall, but as soon as he turned the corner he pumped his fist and then raced down the hall to his room. *A year early*, he thought excitedly. As talented as Gabriel was, he had only entered the advanced program six months early. He would show everyone that he was more talented and more trustworthy than his brother ever was. When people talked about the Knights, they would talk of David's honor and talent, not the treason of his family.

Fifty-Eight

From the uppermost branches of a tall pine more than a mile away, Gabriel had a clear view of the Warrior's Plateau. His superhuman eyes zoomed in on the location, watching for any signs of movement. His plan was to be the last to the party. Arriving early would only allow his enemies the opportunity to sneak up on him. He needed to know what and who he was dealing with before he went in, especially now that he was planning a more aggressive approach.

A slight movement caught his eye. A lone angel had crept into view. She was scaling the plateau from the east, climbing silently, cautiously. *A scout*, he thought.

Upon reaching the pinnacle, she peeked over the edge, surveying the broad area before her. It was an empty wasteland; not a single plant, animal, or even insect occupied the space. Satisfied that she was the first to arrive, she raised a small radio to her lips—she was most likely relaying the information back to Dionysus. The rest of the posse would arrive soon.

Sure enough, within minutes Gabriel spotted a—for lack of a better word—*flock* of angels riding the gentle breeze along the horizon. Characteristically, they were in a perfect V-formation, with a lead angel, followed by pairs of secondary angels. Each pair was spread further apart than the previous pair. There were also several angels clustered in the middle of the formation.

When they got closer, Gabriel could make out some of the faces. He couldn't believe his eyes—the middle of the formation was made up of Archangels! Johanna, Sarah, Thomas—he counted them off on his fingers. He was up to nine when he noticed Dionysus in the very center. *Ten.* Andrew, of course, was dead. *Who was missing?* Then it dawned on him: Michael.

Why would Dionysus's biggest advocate and second-in-command not participate? Gabriel's focused brain cycled through the possible reasons: One—Michael would be part of a trap, arriving later. Gabriel hoped that wasn't the reason. Two—Michael was dead. Not likely, but one can hope, right? Three—in case something went wrong, they would need someone to lead the angels, that someone being Michael. Possible, but Dionysus was such an optimist that Gabriel doubted he had a contingency plan for anything.

That's all he could come up with off the top of his head. His instincts told him that one of the answers was right, but he couldn't quite put his finger on it. Probably the trap; he would need to keep his eyes open.

The pack reached the plateau and descended gracefully. Their positioning was simple: ten guards in a line, not including several hovering in the air, then the ten Archangels behind them, with Dionysus in the center, five on one side, four on the other. *But where was his family?*

As if in response to his question, his family appeared instantly, just behind the line of Archangels. Gabriel rubbed his eyes. When he opened them again, his family was still there. They were holding hands with each other. Peter was in the middle, holding both his mom's and dad's hands, but there was also a fourth, darker figure that was holding Helena's other hand. Upon closer inspection Gabriel saw that they weren't choosing to hold hands, rather they were shackled together. Even from a mile away, Gabriel knew the fourth figure was a demon; a demon who had teleported them onto the plateau; a demon that had switched sides.

Gabriel knew that Dionysus would have something up his sleeve, but this was completely unexpected. There was no doubt that Dionysus had instructed the demon to teleport the prisoners away at the first sign of trouble. This was going to be a problem. He would have to find a way to get close enough to his mom to unshackle her from the demon.

Oh well, Gabriel thought, *he had no choice but to enter the dragon's lair.* As the sun began to melt onto the horizon, Gabriel sprang from his perch and soared towards the plateau.

Fifty-Nine

Gabriel covered the mile in mere seconds and was nearly on top of them before the angels noticed his arrival. Expecting an attack, the guards raised their swords and gritted their teeth. Instead, Gabriel landed softly in front of them, ignoring their threatening gestures. He looked past the guards to the Archangels, and then on to his family.

His eyes returning to Dionysus, he said, "Why don't you just let them go. They have nothing to do with this."

Dionysus laughed. It was more of a cackle really—a long, drawn out, particularly evil-sounding cackle that told Gabriel it was definitely not going to be that easy.

"I'll take that as a no," Gabriel said. "It couldn't hurt to ask."

"I will be dictating the terms of this transaction," Dionysus said succinctly. He made it sound like a standard business deal. To him, it probably was. "First, I would like to draw your attention to the demon that is shackled to your parents." The demon raised his arm, lifting Helena Knight's limb by default. "He has orders to teleport your entire family away if you try anything stupid…So do us all a favor, and don't try anything stupid."

"Hi, Gabriel," Helena said evenly.

"Hi, Mom, Dad, Peter. Are you all okay?"

"We're fine, Gabriel," Teddy said. He added quickly, "Don't worry about us, just leave now!"

Dionysus took one step back and with impressive speed, landed a wicked back-hand slap across Teddy's cheekbone. His father's head snapped back and then rebounded, jerking forward violently. He winced in pain as a trickle of blood originated from a cut just under his eye. With his powerful vision, Gabriel could see that Dionysus was wearing rings on both hands, which is what likely caused the skin to tear. He considered lunging forward and trying to break through the guards to get to Dionysus, but thought better of it and restrained himself.

Instead, he said, "Wow, impressive. Attacking an unarmed, defenseless human…I can see why they made you the leader." The sarcasm was heavy in his tone.

Ignoring the jab, Dionysus threatened, "I would be happy to do a lot worse to the parents that raised their son to be a massive traitor to his people. But that's not part of the plan today unless you want it to be," he added.

"No!" Gabriel blurted out. While he didn't want to cooperate with the vile creature before him, he had to be careful not to push him too far.

"Good." Picking up where he had left off earlier, Dionysus said, "Second, we didn't just bring you to this place because we thought the view was nice, we brought you here for a purpose. For a game, you might say." He paused for effect, but Gabriel remained stone-faced, trying to appear unsurprised by anything that the madman threw at him. "Where was I? Ah, yes, a game! Many years ago the angels and demons held tests of hand-to-hand combat skills here. I would like to renew that tradition today."

"And what if I refuse to fight?" Gabriel asked, knowing full-well that he would have to fight.

"Then you die." The head of the Archangels croaked out the last word, making death sound even worse than it is, if that's possible. "But I think you *will* want to fight the angel that has volunteered."

"Let me guess: tall, full of himself, fights like a girl? I think his name was Pucas. No wait, that's not right, it was Lucas."

Dionysus was not amused by Gabriel's wit. "Enough talk. Bring in the warrior!" he roared.

From behind Gabriel's family, Lucas rose from the cliffs below, his wings beating gracefully. Wearing full body armor, Lucas looked impenetrable compared to Gabriel's exposed skin. After flying over the heads of the Archangels and guards, Lucas hovered for a moment, and then retracted his wings, landing in a low crouch like a ninja. "We meet again. I said we would," Lucas sneered.

"Well, aren't you just a regular walking, talking damn psychic," Gabriel taunted.

Lucas began walking forward towards Gabriel, but Dionysus stopped him with a sharp, "Not yet!" Frozen in his tracks, Lucas waited dumbly. "We have another surprise for you, traitor."

Great, Gabriel thought.

"Bring in Lucas's apprentice!" Dionysus commanded.

Following the same path that Lucas had, a pair of bright forms rose up, just as the last rays of sun beamed across the valley. Temporarily blinded by the sudden burst of light, Gabriel couldn't quite make out the faces of the beings. He could tell that one was tall with long hair, presumably a female, and the other was shorter, but not by much. As he shielded his eyes with a hand, Gabriel heard his mom scream, "Noo! David, what are you doing?"

His heart sank. This explained why Dionysus had told him that David would not be joining his family. He had been kidnapped and was probably being brainwashed already. The sun sank below the horizon, and Gabriel saw the cold face of his brother, who had now landed behind

Lucas but in front of the guards. Their stares locked, and while Gabriel's eyes softened, David's remained hard and emotionless.

"David, I—"

"Shut it!" David's escort ordered. Distracted by David's sudden appearance, Gabriel hadn't noticed who was holding the boy's hand, leading him onto the rock. *Another surprise.* It was Cassandra. As her blond hair swished gently on the breeze, her lips formed into an ugly sneer. While some men would consider her devastatingly beautiful, Gabriel could only see her as ugly. Pure evil filled the hole where her heart used to be. Gabriel remembered a time when they had been friends, good friends even. But those times were long past and Cassandra would always resent Gabriel for not wanting to take their relationship past the friendship stage. Now she was glaring at him.

Helena broke the silence caused by Cassandra's outburst. "David, why are you doing this?" she pleaded.

Looking back, David said, "If you love Gabriel, you will cooperate. This is the only way we can save him." Turning his head back to Gabriel, he said firmly, "Turn yourself in, brother. We can help you. I can help you. Please listen to me."

Gabriel looked to the heavens for an answer of some kind, but hearing nothing, just said, "David, you don't know what you're talking about. You have the story all wrong and if you just stay with Mom and Dad, they'll tell you the truth. I will save you all."

"No, Gabriel, you won't. You'll contaminate us with your filth. They said you would try to lie, but please don't. No more lies. Just turn yourself in."

Gabriel was rattled. This was *not* his brother. Not the innocent boy he had climbed trees and played football with. Not the boy who had looked up to him, who wanted to be like him. This was a robot, a product of Dionysus's darkest thoughts. He was not going to convince David today, not now. Maybe never. Focus. Focus. Focus.

Suddenly he was angry. Ravenously angry. Dangerously angry. Angry enough to kill. He leapt at Lucas, simultaneously drawing his sword. The swiftness of his attack was unexpected, and Lucas was unable to protect himself. With a flash of light, Gabriel's searing white sword slashed across Lucas's chest plate. The armor probably saved his life, because Gabriel's strike was so precise, so powerful, that the steel tore in half as easily as if it were nothing more than paper.

Although he was still wearing arm and leg guards, Lucas's chest was now exposed, significantly evening the fight. After being knocked back, Lucas had drawn his sword and leapt to his feet, recovering quickly.

Gabriel risked a glance at David. Cassie had pushed him behind her protectively, but Gabriel could see that his brother was watching the fight with wide eyes.

Lucas charged, his face seething with rage, but Gabriel managed to side step and avoid the attack while, at the same time, using his fist to fire two small light orbs at his opponent. Lucas took one in the chest and the other in the shoulder. Grunting with pain he went down hard, crashing to the ground in a heap.

Just to keep things fair, Cassie jumped into the fray, slashing viciously with two small daggers. Gabriel was able to deflect her first five strokes with his sword, but the sixth snuck through and glanced off of his left bicep, producing a foot-long gash. Taking a moment to inspect the wound—it was not too deep, merely a flesh wound, as they say—Gabriel was unaware of Lucas, who had regained his feet, circling in behind him.

A sixth-sense alerted him to the attack. It came from both sides, with Cassie whipping her short swords around like batons and Lucas stabbing at him from the back. Just before Lucas's sword would have impaled him, Gabriel ducked sharply and thrust his sword upwards with both hands, simultaneously blocking a two-sword attack from Cassie. Metal clanged on metal.

Next, Gabriel rolled to the side out of harm's way, and then fired ten rounds of light orbs at each of his attackers. While both Cassie and Lucas were ready for the counterattack and easily blocked the balls of light with their weapons, the distraction gave Gabriel the opportunity to rush to David. When he tried to pick his brother up to fly him away, David squirmed free and swiped at Gabriel's leg.

At first Gabriel didn't understand what had happened. Why would his brother punch him in the leg? *Then he felt the pain.* Looking down, the white blood was already pooling at his feet. A black knife had been thrust into his thigh—a demon's knife. *David must have been hiding it up his sleeve or beneath his robe,* he thought. Reaching down, Gabriel tried to wrench the sharp metal from his flesh, but it wouldn't budge. Already he could feel the demon magic working its way through his blood.

A demon knife was an incapacitator, not a killer. Eventually, the demon poison would arrest his heart and brain, sending him into a coma-like trance that would sideline him for at least a week. So this was Dionysus's plan: use his own brother against him to capture him. He felt violated, cheated.

He had five minutes—maybe ten if he could generate enough adrenaline to dilute the poison—before he would be weakened beyond recovery. He needed to make the most of it. Fight or flight? With his family at stake, he would surely fight.

Sixty

"Why don't we just go in now?" Taylor asked anxiously. She was watching Gabriel speak to Dionysus. She was perched on a nearby cliff, using binoculars to get a clear view of the action. Kiren and Sampson were doing the same and were waiting for Chris's signal to teleport in.

Chris said, "Because we need to ensure we have a clear picture of the situation. It's my guess that Dionysus will have a few more tricks up his sleeve that he has not yet revealed." They had already discussed the situation with the demon being tethered to the Knights. To deal with it, Chris would have to perform a pinpoint teleport—landing practically on top of the demon—and then teleport them all away while trying to kill or incapacitate the demon. It sounded impossible.

Taylor continued watching nervously. It was hard for her to stand by and watch while Gabriel stood alone against at least twenty angels. But she would try to trust Chris.

Soon enough, they found out his guess was right.

They watched as first Lucas and then Cassie and David made their appearance. "Damn, that's Gabriel's brother, David. I met him once. Why is he with that witch, Cassie?" Taylor wondered aloud. "What are they saying, Sampson?"

Sampson tilted his highly-sensitive ear towards the action and listened for a few minutes. "You don't want to know, Taylor."

"Tell me anyway."

Grudgingly, Sampson said, "David is now Lucas's apprentice. He believes Gabriel is a traitor and needs to be taken by the angels to be helped."

"But that's crazy, David adores Gabriel!"

"Not anymore. He's been brainwashed."

"Wait a minute, the fight's starting!" Chris yelled.

"Teleport me," Taylor insisted.

"Not yet, let's wait and see what happens first. We only have one chance at using the element of surprise to our advantage. Let's not waste it."

Taylor pumped her fist a few times as Gabriel began winning the fight. When Cassie doubled up on him, she said again, "Chris, can we please go now?"

"Not yet," he replied flatly.

They saw Gabriel perform a brilliant move to avoid a duel-attack and then watched in astonishment as he raced for David. "He's going to rescue him!" Taylor yelled. And then: "What the—? What happened?"

Sampson, whose normal eyesight was even better than those who were using binoculars, said glumly, "David stabbed him. It was a demon knife."

"Oh no," Chris said.

"Dammit, Chris! Can we go NOW!" Taylor demanded.

"Yes, now is the time," Chris confirmed. "Change of plans, guys. I will teleport Taylor and then leave her. She will distract everyone—I think we can be sure of that. Kiren—two minutes after I leave Taylor, you guys teleport into the midst of the Council and hit anyone you can. I will follow you and grab Gabriel's family."

"What about an escape plan?" Sampson asked urgently.

"We'll probably have to play it by ear, but I will be gone already, so Kiren will have to be responsible for getting Gabriel and Taylor out, unless I can get back fast enough. Sampson, if you're able to teleport out with them, do it, but if not, you'll just have to fly back to the Lair like a bat out of hell. Let's go!" Taylor was still processing everything he had said when Chris grabbed her hand. Faster than she could blink, they were gone.

Sixty-One

Gabriel lay on the ground, pretending to writhe in pain. Sure, it hurt, but not so much that he couldn't stand up. In his peripheral vision he could see Lucas approaching— there was a cockiness in his stride. He probably thought that Gabriel would be in a coma soon, the battle already over.

But not to Gabriel. As he lay on the ground, he was desperately charging up his body for his final stand.

When Lucas got within a yard of him, Gabriel suddenly pointed both hands at him and fired off a single, massive light orb. Lucas raised his sword to try to block the attack, but the force was too powerful. His sword shattered into a thousand tiny pieces, spraying him with metal shrapnel. The orb crashed into his chest, launching him backwards fifty yards.

Using a karate-style leap to regain his feet, Gabriel turned his attention to Cassie, who was now crouched, her teeth bared. She hissed at him like an animal. He sprang at her, swinging his sword with reckless abandon, as if it were as light as a toothpick. After a dozen lightning-quick strokes, Gabriel had disarmed her and had the point of his sword pointed at her neck. "I win," he growled. "Give me my family."

"Bravo! Bravo, Gabriel!" Dionysus said, clapping slowly as he passed through his line of guards. "I really didn't think you had it in you. Unfortunately, I can't satisfy your request. You see, the duel was just for my own amusement and you know as well as I do that I was never going to let your family go."

Gabriel's legs suddenly froze up and he nearly toppled over. Using his sword as a cane he was barely able to maintain his balance. Seizing the opportunity, Cassie rolled away and retrieved her weapons. Rapidly, she stuck one to his exposed neck. Gabriel could see the fury in her eyes—her animal instincts were likely urging her to finish him off.

"Stop!" a female voice yelled.

All eyes shifted to see who the newcomer was who would dare to interrupt them. Taylor approached boldly, her eyes forward, her chin held high. Her confidence was not an act. Her anger had emboldened her. Chris was already gone.

Dionysus's lips curled into a smile. "Ahh, my dear. Welcome. I'd like to say it is a pleasure to see you, but considering you killed a hundred of my people the last time I saw you…Well, I guess that's in the past, water under the bridge as they say. What brings you to our little gathering?"

"I have an offer to make you."

"I'm listening."

"Me…for Gabriel and his family."

"Taylor, no!" Gabriel groaned. He was lying on the ground now, his body slowly succumbing to the poison that was working its way relentlessly through his bloodstream.

Ignoring the fallen angel, Dionysus gazed curiously at Taylor, as if he didn't know what to make of her. "Hmm," he mused, "an interesting proposition. But what's to stop me from just grabbing you now and taking all of you?"

"Trust me, that won't work. How do you think I got here? I can get out just as easily and quickly." She maintained a safe enough distance that he had no choice but to believe her.

"I accept your offer," Dionysus confirmed. "How will this work?"

"No, Taylor, don't do this," Gabriel croaked. His voice was becoming weaker.

"For starters, you can get the damn sword off of his neck," Taylor said through clenched teeth. Ignoring the request, Cassie hissed at Taylor, like an animal protecting her kill.

"Now, now, Cassie. Do as she says." Cassie looked up, surprised, but then obeyed her master. She backed away from Gabriel.

Taylor had been silently counting in her head ever since Chris had dropped her off. *110 seconds had elapsed; phase two would begin any second.*

Trying to buy a little more time, she said firmly, "Okay, here's how it's gonna work. First, you cut that demon away from the Knights. Then, you bring them over here with Gabriel and back away from them. I will come over and hold your hand." She motioned to Dionysus. "I've got a guy who will come in and retrieve the Knights and then you will have your prize."

They couldn't have possibly timed it any better. The moment that Taylor said *prize*, there was a scream of agony from Felix, one of the younger Archangels.

All eyes shifted to Felix, who fell to his knees, his face contorted in pain. The black tip of a fiery blade protruded slightly from his chest. When he dropped to the ground the attacker was revealed—it was Kiren. Deftly, she pulled the sword from her prey and swung it sharply at the next Archangel, Johanna.

Eyes blazing with anger, Johanna had already drawn her sword and easily deflected the blow. Just as the other Archangels, including Dionysus, moved to surround the lone demon warrior, the next surprise appeared. Sampson swooped in from directly above Dionysus, where he had been in a free fall. Just before teleporting behind Felix, Kiren had evidently teleported Sampson high in the air over the plateau. While she began the fight he was able to use gravity as an escort, while remaining undetected by those on the ground.

Immediately before impact, he spread his wings and careened into Dionysus, knocking him hard to the ground. Dionysus groaned, as the collision took its toll. Only surprised for a few moments, the Archangels quickly recovered and launched themselves into a full counterattack on the angel-demon pair. Only Dionysus was careful to keep an eye on Gabriel, who was pinned to the ground, and Taylor, who was speaking to him softly. No one except the lone demon guard was watching the Knights.

Chris appeared next to the demon guard with his sword already out, but he didn't use it. Instead, he grabbed the surprised demon's arm and teleported him, along with the Knights—who were tied to him—back to the Elders room, where a surprised group of demon Elders were conducting a meeting.

A gasp arose as the unexpected and strange group of visitors appeared. "What is the meaning of this?" Clifford barked.

Ignoring him, Chris aimed his sword in the direction of the demon's arm and swung hard. Just in time, the demon used his other hand to grab Chris's wrist and force the sword away from its intended mark. At the same time, the demon guard teleported them back to the Warrior's Plateau.

※

Taylor was about to yell to Sampson and Kiren to tell them that Chris had escaped with the Knights, when she saw Gabriel's family reappear in the exact same spot where they had been originally. *This is not good*, she thought, as she watched the battle continue. Sampson and Kiren were hopelessly outnumbered and the element of surprise was quickly fading.

Chris seemed to be locked in a wrestling match with the demon traitor, and she watched in awe as they disappeared again, only to reappear seconds later, still fighting. This happened several more times as each side tried to gain an advantage. They popped in and out of view like the light from a dying light bulb.

Chris had expected his opponent to try to teleport them back to the fight, but he had hoped to prevent it by cutting him free from the Knights. The demon's quick reflexes were able to stop Chris's first attempt, but with only one free hand—the other was tied to Helena Knight—Chris was slowly gaining an advantage. Each time one of them teleported the group of prisoners, Chris was able to slowly force the demon's right hand down towards his side.

By about the fifth teleport, Chris was able to use just his left arm to subdue his opponent's only free arm, freeing up his own right arm to go on the attack. When the demon attempted a last-ditch teleport to bring them back to the plateau one more time, Chris's right arm flashed across his body and downwards, slashing his sword through the demon's arm, severing it at the wrist.

The demon's face exploded in agony, as torturing pain must have shot through the stump of an arm that remained. He fell to the ground, away from the Knights. Without hesitation, Chris grabbed Helena Knight and teleported her and her family back to the Lair for the last time.

When Taylor saw Chris separate the demon from the Knights and teleport them away, she yelled, "They're out!" Her intention was to signal to Kiren and Sampson that it was time to make their escape, but Dionysus, who had been watching her carefully, was also alerted and looked back, finding that his bait had mysteriously disappeared. He sprang into action, rushing towards the helpless Gabriel.

Kiren and Sampson turned in the direction of Taylor's voice, but it was too late. Dionysus had the tip of his sword under Gabriel's chin. All semblance of his typical snide and sarcastic demeanor was gone and in its place was an expression of pure anger and hatred. His piercing eyes glared at Kiren and Sampson. "Your fun is over," he declared. "One move and he's dead. I am taking them both."

While he spoke, the Archangels and their guards surrounded Kiren and Sampson, and moved to disarm them.

Seeing Dionysus one stroke away from killing Gabriel launched a flood of emotions through Taylor's body. Fear of losing him, anger at the evil that stood before her, determination that she would not fail Gabriel: each emotion intermingled with the others until they became one emotion, one she had never felt before. The new emotion created new blood, which now flowed through her veins in a rush of warmth, like she had been hooked up to an IV that filled her with hot, rather than cold, liquid. The new blood bred new cells in her skin and new marrow in her bones.

※

Dionysus watched as her body began to glow. The light became brighter and brighter until it was as bright as any angel. Even as the evening light was darkening into night, the plateau became as bright as if the sun remained high in the sky.

Taylor lifted off of the ground, seemingly defying gravity and her own human boundaries. She hovered for a few seconds, and then with a sharp tearing sound, two magnificent, white wings burst forth from her back and began to glow in unison with the rest of her body. Much like he had many years earlier, Taylor had evolved into something nonhuman; something that could only be described as an angel.

But something was different about her. While angels have an inner light that helps fuel their extraordinary powers, they rely on the power of external light to charge their inner light. Taylor seemed to radiate power from within her, without any assistance from the outside world. In essence, she was her own power source.

Dionysus recognized something in her face, in her glowing frame. Sensing danger, he cowered behind Gabriel's slumped body.

Initially, Taylor was concerned when she felt her body heating up again, but soon she was overcome by the beautiful tingling sensation. It felt right. Instinct told her that she was about to find her true place in the world. She smiled. Even when wings sprouted from her back, she smiled. She knew what she had to do.

"Get out of here!" she yelled. Before the angels knew what was happening, Kiren, who was in the midst of a circle of angels, teleported to Sampson, and then, quicker than the blink of an eye, teleported them both away. With Chris and the Knights also gone, only Taylor and Gabriel remained. *Just a couple of roses amongst the thorns,* Taylor thought. She was still smiling.

She could tell that Dionysus recognized the gleam in her eyes. Even as she fired her weapon, he was yelling, "FLYYYYY!"

A heavy beam of light burst from Taylor's outstretched hands, colliding with the group of Archangels and angel guards, immediately vaporizing them. A lucky few were able to react to Dionysus's scream fast enough and shot into the sky and away from Taylor, racing back towards the angels' mountain.

During the melee, Cassie had evidently taken it upon herself to protect David Knight, and now stood on the edge of the plateau with her arm around the boy. Her mouth gaped open at the sight of the destruction caused by the human girl. Like a statue, she was frozen in place. Before Taylor could aim again, Dionysus ran to Cassie and David, picked each of them up with a different arm, and soared into the evening sky.

Taylor's first instinct was to chase them, to finish what she had started. The energy pulsing through her veins was intoxicating. She felt powerful, invincible, as she continued to hover in the air, her wings instinctively waving up and down using some new muscle. Her senses were heightened as well. She could see a bat sliding noiselessly through the air. She watched, mesmerized that she was able to ascertain the most intricate details of its tiny wings. The texture, the color, even the veins. And she could hear its breathing, shallow and quick. A strange throbbing sound pulsed in her eardrum. What was that? It hit her—it was the bat's heartbeat. *Amazing! Then she realized that the bat was at least ten mountains to the west, probably about five miles away.*

All of these thoughts went through Taylor's brain in mere seconds, as even her ability to think was heightened. She found that she could now process thousands of sensory and logical inputs simultaneously.

Someone groaned.

Abruptly, her wings retracted and she dropped to the ground, landing easily on both feet. Gabriel looked like he was dying; his face was ashen and his eyes closed. In reality, he was slipping into a coma, a result of the demon blade that David had pushed deep into his leg. But Taylor didn't know that. She just thought that she was about to lose the only thing that truly mattered in her world.

But somehow she knew that she could help him. Placing her still-glowing hands on his head, she moved her lips as if to speak, but said nothing. Her hands brightened. The light from her hands was seemingly transfused into Gabriel's head, and then crept slowly along his scalp, onto his cheeks, down his neck, and along his bare chest. The knife popped out of his leg and thumped to the ground, scattering dust particles.

It was a day of extremes. Unexpectedly, Taylor felt weak, like she was sick with a bad case of the flu. Unable to hold herself up to even kneel, she toppled over and lay on the ground, breathing heavily. *Was she dying?* Or maybe she was already dead. She couldn't have possibly become an angel unless she was dead.

Gabriel groaned again, but this time it was different. Not an I-think-I-might-be-dying kind of groan like before, but more like an I-was-hurt-but-might-be-recovering type of groan. Taylor tried to lift her head to look at him, but couldn't seem to find the strength.

She heard, "Taylor, Taylor?" A hand shook her. She opened her eyes to see Gabriel's beautiful blue eyes looking at her anxiously. "Are you hurt, Taylor?"

"I don't think so, just tired," she replied.

A relieved smile crossed Gabriel's face. "What happened?"

"I'm not really sure exactly. And if I told you, I don't think you'd believe me anyway."

"My family?"

"Fine, I think. Back at the Lair. Chris saved them."

"And David?"

Taylor frowned. She shook her head. "With Dionysus," she said simply.

A sudden memory seemed to flash across Gabriel's face, his eyes widening. He said, "David—he cut me. It was a demon's blade. I feel great, but how?"

"I think I healed you."

Gabriel gazed at his girlfriend in awe. "Just when I think you can't surprise me anymore…," he said. "You'll have to tell me all about it later, once you've rested."

"I will, I promise."

Gabriel reached out and touched Taylor's head. "Taylor, your hair," he said.

"What?" He lifted a lock of Taylor's hair and moved it in front of her face so she could see it. It was white. Frantically, Taylor grabbed a handful of her hair and pulled it in front of her eyes. Still good old brown, thank God. *Strange*, she thought. "Just one lock?" she asked.

Gabriel nodded. Taylor wondered what other changes she had undergone. She started to get up, but Gabriel stopped her. "Taylor, I think you need to rest."

"I'm fine. Really," she insisted.

Gabriel helped her to her feet. Taylor was feeling strong again already. If she was really an angel, then she would recover much quicker than when she was a human.

At that moment, dozens of demons began appearing around them, one by one. There was one human, too. "Sam!" Taylor exclaimed.

Sam approached them, holding Chris's hand. "Thank you for not dying, Tay," she said with a smile. The best friends embraced; their hug was long and warm. A little more warm than Sam expected. "Taylor, are you feeling alright? You're burning up."

"You didn't tell her?" Taylor asked Kiren, who had just approached the group.

"Tell her what?" Sam, Gabriel, and Chris said simultaneously.

Kiren shrugged. "I thought you would want to do it yourself."

Looking embarrassed, Taylor said, "Well, the thing is...it's kind of a funny story, really. It seems that I might not be... fully...human...anymore."

Gabriel was looking at her strangely, like he didn't understand. Sam, on the other hand, seemed to recognize the truth immediately. "Let me see your wings!" she said in excitement.

Still looking sheepish, Taylor put her arms around Gabriel's neck and kissed him on the lips. When she pulled away, she asked, "If I show you something, do you promise not to run away screaming?" Her words were identical to the words he had used not so long ago when he showed her something miraculous.

"I promise," he said.

The words had barely escaped his lips before her beautiful brand new fifth and sixth appendages shot from her back and extended over her head. They shimmered in the moonlight, as if a million diamonds covered them.

"Wow!" Sam exclaimed. "They're perfect. And I like the hair, too. It fits in with your punk look."

Despite being ready to witness the impossible, Gabriel appeared awestruck. "Tay, they're amazing." He walked over to inspect them.

"No better than any other angels' wings," Taylor noted.

Gabriel ran his hand along the feathers. "Actually, I think they're far superior to any wings I've seen before."

"What do you mean?"

"They're different than mine. They seem bigger and stronger, yet lighter than other angels' wings. Here, let me show you." With a pop, Gabriel's own set of beautiful wings extended. He compared them to hers. Next to Taylor's, his wings seemed basic and boring, like the old model of a newly redesigned car.

"Wow!" Sam said again. "Yours are so much nicer. No offense, Gabriel."

"But why?" Taylor asked.

"I don't have the slightest idea," Gabriel said. "It almost seems like a miracle."

Sixty-Two

The last three days had been peaceful. Sure, there were massive celebration parties, dozens of meetings, and plenty of games of pool, but compared to the last week it couldn't have been any more relaxing. There was also a lot of catching up to do. Gabriel introduced Taylor to his family members and they immediately welcomed her as a friend. They had already seen her dedication to Gabriel when she willingly offered to sacrifice herself to save him. A few tears were shed when they talked about David and the choices he had made, but overall the feeling amongst Taylor and her friends was happiness, pure and unchained.

Clifford, of course, requested a full briefing of the events. Upon meeting with the Elders, the first part of the story was told by the Knights, who were the only eye witnesses to their own abduction. Next, Gabriel picked up the story from his rescue attempt to the point where he blacked out. Then, the Elders and their guests all listened in fascination while Taylor recounted the rest of the incredible story. Initially, Clifford was angry for being disobeyed, but when he recognized the extreme bravery that they had all demonstrated, he was quick to forgive and forget.

"Extraordinary. Absolutely extraordinary," he said. "This is only the third example of significant human evolution in the last two thousand years. First, the Demon Evolution. Then, the Angel Evolution. Now, this. I don't even know what to call it. We will have to study her."

"Not so fast, Dr. Frankenstein," Gabriel interjected. "She's not some kind of lab rat, you know."

"It's okay, Gabriel," Taylor said. "I'm willing to have a few tests run to see what can be learned from me. I'm curious myself."

"As long as I am present for all tests," Gabriel demanded.

"Of course, of course," Clifford said, throwing his hands up defensively. "There will be time to discuss the details. For now, I just want to congratulate you all on what you have accomplished. We all believed it was a dire situation, one that would likely result in the loss of many lives. While that is true, they were all enemy lives and thanks to Taylor, the angel leadership has never been weaker. They have lost many Archangels."

Taylor squirmed in her seat. She wasn't comfortable with the fact that she had killed so many angels…again. It seemed like every few days her weapon caused many deaths. It wasn't that she believed her actions were unjustified, because she knew they were. She just hated thinking about it; it made her nauseous.

Clifford continued: "In any case, in just a few days our guests of honor, Taylor and Samantha, will be leaving us."

"What?!" Taylor yelled. "I'm an angel now, I'm not going anywhere."

"My dear, I appreciate your position, but you still have a human family. And until they know the truth, you still have obligations to them."

Taylor had forgotten about her father. But how could she tell her dad something this big? *Hi, Dad, I'm home! I had a great time playing pool, hanging out with Sam, and oh, by the way, I saved the demons from destruction and evolved into an angel while I was away, too.* Not a conversation she was itching to have anytime soon. She knew Clifford was right.

"Okay, but will we be safe?" She said "we", but really she meant Sam. Now that Taylor was an angel, and a powerful one at that, she felt like she could protect herself.

"We are planning on giving you some really good escorts, you might know them. Gabriel and Chris will be attending UT with you next semester."

Taylor smiled, and happiness filled her. Looking down the table at Sam she could see that her friend was feeling the same way—she was absolutely beaming, her arm wrapped around Christopher. Taylor turned back to Gabriel who had put his arm around her; she stretched up to kiss him. As their lips met, she heard the applause of the entire panel of Elders. She knew that not only were they cheering for her and for Gabriel, but also for the fact that good had prevailed once again.

She began to daydream of the next few months: being back at school with Gabriel, lazy days on the school lawn, skipping class and playing pool with her friends. Maybe going back to the human world was just what she needed. A relaxing semester at college with the love of her life and her friends sounded pretty good all of a sudden.

If only.

Sixty-Three

"DAMMIT!!!" he roared, tossing tables, chairs and anything else he could get his hands on across the room. Each piece of furniture that he launched smashed against the wall or the floor and crumbled on impact.

David seemed to be cowering in the corner, while Cassandra did her best to protect him from the carnage. Three other Archangels were trying to subdue their leader. They were the last living Archangels. "Calm yourself, Dionysus," Johanna said firmly. "You're scaring the boy."

For some reason, these words got his attention. In mid-throw, he froze, a plush, white ottoman dangling from his fingers over his head. Dionysus gazed across the room at the boy, who was a miniature version of his greatest enemy. "Ahh, David," he said soothingly. "I'm sorry I lost my temper, David."

David peeked out from behind Cassie. "No problem, my lord. I understand." To everyone's surprise, David was calm and collected. He didn't look scared at all. On the contrary, his face was confident, emotionless.

Pacified, Dionysus asked, "What do you make of all of this, David?"

"It was a bad loss, my lord. Probably the worst we have ever seen. But all is not lost. We can still prevail." His voice sounded older somehow.

Dionysus marveled at the strength of the young boy. He had the same strength that he had seen in Gabriel long ago, the same strength that he saw in himself. "You are wise, David. What must we do?"

David didn't seem surprised that Dionysus was asking his opinion on strategy. It was like he had matured ten years over the course of the day. He was changed, somehow. "We must crush them."

The boy said it with such malice, such contempt, that even Dionysus felt an involuntary shudder pass through him. Dionysus smiled. "We will crush them, David. And you will help us do it."

Discover other books by David Estes at:
http://davidestesbooks.blogspot.com

The Evolution Trilogy
Book One—Angel Evolution
Book Two—Demon Evolution
Book Three—Archangel Evolution

About the Author

After growing up in Pittsburgh, Pennsylvania, David Estes moved to Sydney, Australia where he lives with his wife Adele. When he's not writing, he's enjoying the sun and surf at Manly Beach.

Made in the USA
Charleston, SC
01 February 2013